Sons of the Sea

Stanley McShane

DEDICATION

"To my Grandfather and my old shipmates of Grimsby"

All "SONS OF THE SEA" – Patrick John Rose

This book is additionally dedicated to the family of Patrick John "Stanley McShane" Rose.

Stanley McShane is the author of <u>Bitter River Ranch</u> (Phoenix Press - 1936), <u>Cocos Island Treasure</u> and <u>Lucky Joe</u> (Rose Point Publishing- 2012). <u>Cocos Island Treasure</u> and <u>Lucky Joe</u> can currently be found on Amazon.com and in digital form through Kindle and Barnes & Noble.

Illustrations :
Grimsby Seaport, England
Dacre Castle, Cumbria, England
Dogger Banks, North Sea
Ship Diagram
Cover Design by Christine Armstrong

CONTENTS

ACKNOWLEDGMENTS

When Grandpa Rose left me his old trunk filled with his treasured manuscripts, photos, mementoes, clippings, 8 x 10 pasteboard paintings and photos of his paintings created to illustrate his books written in the politically incorrect late 1920's, he also gave me strict instructions on how to retype and submit them. I am confident he never could have envisioned the technology which would make those instructions archaic as well as cost prohibitive and these days actually inaccurate. Today, thanks to such self-publishing giants as Amazon.com, his manuscripts can be published posthumously and distributed among his heirs and interested fans more than 80 years after they were written. If you are reading this as a paperback novel or in digital form—then I've finally fulfilled my promise to submit his works for publication and believe he'd approve.

His granddaughter—Virginia Williams

Grimsby seaport, 6 miles from the North Sea.

The **Humber** is a large tidal estuary on the east coast of Northern England. Ports on the Humber include Kingston upon Hull (better known as simply Hull), Grimsby, Immingham, New Holland and Killingholme. The estuary is navigable here for the largest of deep-sea vessels.*

The estuary itself is more than 0.75 mile (1.2 km) across at its farthest inland point and widens to more than 7 miles (11 km) near its mouth; there Spurn Head, a sand and shingle spit with lighthouse, lifeboat station, and bird sanctuary, extends into the estuary.**

*http://en.wikipedia.org/wiki/Humber
**http://www.britannica.com/EBchecked/topic/276044/River-Humber

Grimsby, England
Grimsby; seaport, Lincolnshire, eastern England

1
THE BELLE OF GRIMSBY

From her bedroom window Edith Virginia Moresby had sighted the fishing fleet as it rounded Spurn Head Lighthouse into the mouth of the Humber. She laid aside her late grandfather's telescope and, after a hasty glance into the mirror, hurried away with a song on her lips.

Less than a half hour later, she stood on the smelly, fishy wharf wrinkling up her lovely nose. The southeast wind rippled her long, golden tresses and the white costume she wore that day emphasizing the winsome, youthful contours of her figure.

Sea gulls whirled and soared above her. They anticipated a great feed of fish on that sunny afternoon. They flew out to the boats and then back again to the wharf, circling about with raucous cries. The girl was not interested in them. She was watching a blue pennant with its cross of white rise up to the masthead—a pennant that she had made for Captain Beasley, whose chrome-green eyes clouded at times with a hint of mystery or sorrow, had stirred her curiosity.

Captain Beasley was watching the girl through his binoculars. Unclouded now, his eyes sparkled as he turned to his mate and friend, Victor Jenson, a man whose life he had saved up in the North Sea off the Dogger Banks, during a raging northeaster a month before.

"The night before we left port, Victor, I asked Edith if she wouldn't like to see the fleet heading out to sea from that very wharf where she's standing now, and she told me she could see the ships better from her bedroom window without having to smell those noisome, fishy odors

1

on the wharf. Can you beat it? There the darling is—waiting for us!" He chuckled, as he raised his glasses again, ending, "and in spite of the fish perfume!"

"There she ain't, you mean, Jud!" Victor laughed, as he lowered his binoculars, for he had noted the fact that Edith had waved her handkerchief, turned on her heels and retraced her footsteps from the wharf.

Captain Beasley had noted that fact and lowered his glasses. The light in his eyes went out like a burnt-out match. They were now shrouded in gloom. Victor wondered what his skipper's thoughts were at that moment. He, like all who came in contact with Beasley, believed that the man was nursing some great sorrow. Respecting his friend's silence, he waited for Jud to confide in him. It was nearly a year now since Beasley, born in Boston, Massachusetts thirty years before, had drifted into Grimsby from God only knew where and sought a job from Black Jack Barstow. Barstow was the owner of the fleet and told Jack that he was captain of a fishing schooner sailing out of Gloucester.

As Edith was leaving the wharf she passed by several old fishermen who, seated on boxes and barrels, were mending their nets.

They had spat out a stream of tobacco juice and rose as one, doffing their caps to the girl. She acknowledged their friendly salutations with a smile and a nod of her bonny head and passed on. In her eyes, eyes of turquoise blue, was a merry twinkle as she paused at the office of the company at the head of the wharf and peeked in, hoping to see Black Jack. Asking the bookkeeper if he was in his office and receiving an answer in the negative, she went on out to the street, passing by the Fishermen's Rest, a public house, wrinkling her dainty, sensitive nose in saucy disapproval.

That action of hers had become habitual. It expressed her dislike for fish and the odor of stale beer that emanated from the public houses that she was, at times, compelled to pass.

Reaching the Thornton residence, a two-storied red brick house that stood back a little from the road, she opened the iron gate and passed into the garden where she proceeded to pick some flowers for the parlor vases and to decorate the dining table, for she and her grandmother expected Captain Beasley to dine with them that day.

With an armful of fragrant flowers, she hurried into the house, calling, "Grandma, dear! The fleet is heading in. I saw them from my bedroom window. You were taking a nap when I came downstairs and

I didn't wish to disturb you. I went down to that stinky wharf to watch them. There were no fish there, of course, but, well, I did not stay," she laughed.

"Why not, Edith?" asked the white-haired old lady, whose faded blue eyes glanced up at the girl questioningly.

"Why should I, Grandma? You know that I…….."

"Yes, yes!" interrupted the old woman. "I understand, my dear. You wanted to see just one boat only, Captain Beasley's. Come now, confess." Her grandmother smiled encouragingly as she rose to assist Edith in arranging the flowers.

"Oh, Grandma, what big eyes you've got!" the girl laughed, but more soberly, "you see things that aren't so. I'm merely curious about Captain Beasley. You know as well as I that I shall never marry a smelly fisherman—as my mother did. They lead so dangerous a life that with him up in the North Sea, I would be sobbing my heart out, wondering if I should ever see my husband again. No, Grandma, dear; no fishermen husband for me!" She stamped a foot for emphasis.

She turned to leave the parlor but paused on the threshold and murmured, "I like Jud because he is so different from other men that I've met. Black Jack Barstow and Victor Jenson are both fine men, sons of the sea, fishermen born—fine physiques appealing to the gentle sex; but Jud has more. He has mystery. I can read Black Jack like a book, Grandma. While gentle with the fair sex, I can imagine how domineering he could be. Victor, like his lovely sister, Jenny, are just the opposite. They are both gentle, unassuming and lovable. One can see that in their large, brown eyes—just like their mother's. Victor would let a woman have her own way in all things."

"And so would Captain Beasley—if his wife's name were Edith," suggested the old lady, glancing over the tops of her spectacles as she sat in her chair and picked up her knitting again.

"Perhaps not, Grandma. In those sea-green eyes of his that intrigue me so is a power that neither Black Jack nor Victor possesses. Jud is a leader of men and I dare venture to assume that Black Jack himself, if aboard ship with Captain Beasley, would find out very quickly that he had met his master. But, marriage to a smelly fisherman is the very last thing I am thinking about, believe me."

The buxom old lady smiled again as she said, "The heart of a girl, like the wind, goeth where it listeneth, my child. You, like your mother, Lady Moresby and I, will wed a fisherman."

"Never!" the girl retorted with finality.

Humber
River Humber, North Sea inlet on the east coast of England, one of
the major deepwater estuaries of the United Kingdom.

2
A MAIDEN'S DELIGHT

Jud and Victor sauntered along the wharf in earnest conversation.
Before turning on to the street, Victor laid a hand on Beasley's arm,
"Don't you do it, Jud. I don't care what your hurry is, don't do it! With
them clothes on! You better change before…."

Jud laughed. "Run along home, Victor. It will be all right. I'll be
after you in a jiffy."

He turned off whistling happily and soon Grandma Thornton called
to Edith and informed her that Captain Beasley was outside the gate.
The girl ran upstairs and changed her dress. When the heavy knocker
fell upon the door, Edith ran downstairs and threw the door wide; but
instead of welcoming him home and inviting him in, she stood staring
at him, wrinkling up her nose.

That was the first time he had called at the Thornton residence in
his seagoing clothes. He was speechless. He backed out, sprang over
the gate and hurried home to the Jenson's where he boarded.

"Victor!" he blazed, as he entered the house, "I'm finished! When
Edith opened the door, there she stood—so beautiful my heart stood
still. She didn't move or invite me in, but wrinkled up that nose; that
dainty, sensitive nose of hers that I'd love to kiss."

"What did she say?" asked Victor.

"I'm telling you! That lovely nose of hers spoke volumes. That and
her silence told me quite enough."

Mrs. Jenson entered the room at that moment and welcomed her
boarder home, then told him, "I heard what you said, Judson, but don't

you get to feeling badly about the girl's action. She's forgotten all that by now—but not you. Her grandmother told me that someday she would be marrying a fisherman as her mother did, and that when she leaves St. James Church as a bride, her name will be Mrs. Judson Beasley and not Lady Draker of Dacre Castle at Keswick. But I warn you not to try and rush the girl. Just be patient, son."

"Well, I guess I'll not intrude upon her again tonight. We will leave for Dogger Banks tomorrow, Victor, without casting a weather eye upon her. What do you think of that, Mother Jenson?" asked Jud, winking at his friend.

"Very little, Judson. You will not do anything as foolish. The girl has been looking forward to your return. That is a fact, son. Should you leave port again without seeing her when you return from the North Sea, my lad, that little lady will have flown back to London-and the stage. She and her grandmother are expecting you to dinner."

"Could you—" began Jud, smiling....

"Wait a bit; there's something more, and it's very important. Edith uses a perfume called 'A Maiden's Delight'. I wheedled that information out of her grandmother. You will find a bottle of it on your dressing table, Judson. After bathing, use it likewise."

Victor went out of the house to the garden laughing, but Jud was as sober as a judge. He caught the face of the motherly old lady between his hands and kissed her, telling her she was a treasure. Then he ran up the wooden hill (as Victor called the stairs) to his room. He picked up the bottle of perfume and sniffed it for a few moments then muttered, "It smells damn good!"

He wondered what Edith would have to say about it—if she would be wrinkling up her lovely nose when he entered her home that night. And, a half hour later he ran down the stairs with gleaming eyes, dressed in his shore-going clothes, those of a merchant marine captain. Glancing at Mrs. Jenson as he paused before her, he asked, "Smell fish now, Mother Jenson?"

"How much of that perfume did you use, Jud?" she queried.

"Every blessed drop of it. You can bet I did a good job. I rubbed about four parts of it into my skin after bathing. The rest," he chuckled, "I rubbed into my hair. It smells mighty good to me," he assured her.

"Judson Beasley, you fairly reek of it! If you keep that up you will not have money enough left to pay your board bills. That one bottle should have lasted you a month or more—even if you used it every day. It is very costly."

"Forget it," he smiled. "I'll be admiral of the fleet before long. You know what that will mean? Black Jack Barstow gave me a hint as I left the wharf that when I....."

He hesitated. The glow in his eyes faded. Behind their dullness lurked that mystery that had troubled his friend Victor from the day he had drifted into the port of Grimsby, while Victor and Black Jack were conversing about Jenny's marriage to Captain Robert Boyd, the giant blonde of the fleet. Her marriage had enraged the owner of the fleet for he had long loved Victor's sister, but had waited too long to ask the girl to become his wife. And, to that day, Barstow had never forgotten it.

"I daresay," Mrs. Jenson commented, "that the Belle of Grimsby won't be wrinkling up that nose of hers again this day of our Lord. Run along now and remember my warning, Jud."

"I will that," he said, as he left the house, casting a sly wink at Victor who had entered at that moment.

Outside, he ran into Captain Robert Boyd and his wife Jenny. "Where away?" asked Boyd, his steel grey eyes narrowing.

"Over to the Thornton's to take dinner with the Belle of Grimsby and her grandmother," Jud replied hurriedly, as he walked quickly away down the road.

"I daresay that damned, egotistical Yank thinks he will be taking that lovely little craft in tow some day," Captain Boyd remarked. "I don't. Black Jack Barstow, I heard, had a ripping good time with her while sailing up the Humber. Edith will be going up to the big house on the hill as the bride of the owner of the fleet, my dear."

The Boyds' strolled on up the walk to the Jenson's where they had been invited to dinner.

"Don't be a fool, Bob," Mrs. Boyd remonstrated gently. "Old Lady Barstow told me Edith said, while up there to dinner, that she was leaving for London shortly."

"I know what I know," he grumbled.

Jud had passed through the gate and stood for a moment, thinking. He was about to raise the knocker when the door opened wide. Edith stood smiling at him, wrinkling her nose and sniffing the air.

The glow in Jud's eyes faded again. "Smell fish now?" he blurted.

"No, Jud. Come right in." She added in a whisper as she ushered him in, "Grandma will have something to say to you, I daresay."

Grandma Thornton, dressed in a long, flowing gown of black satin trimmed with lace, at her breast a large cameo brooch studded with a border of small diamonds, rose to greet him. Jud bowed low over her hand as she welcomed him home.

"I think, Captain Beasley," she said, with a sly wink at Edith, "that if all fishermen of the Barstow fleet were as wise as our Yankee Skipper, there would not be a bachelor left in it."

"Meaning, madam?" he queried, glancing from her face to the lovely girl at his side.

"That I notice you have found the means to combat that smelly, fishy odor that my grandchild abhors so. I have only to close my eyes to imagine that all the fragrant flowers in Grimsby had been transported into this parlor. I think you are wonderful, Captain Beasley!"

"Do tell!" he chuckled, while Arabella, the housemaid, stood sniffing the air about her from the threshold for a moment before announcing dinner was served.

"Captain Beasley is a dandy," Arabella said to herself as she turned back to the kitchen, her soft brown eyes aglow. "There will be a pair of dark, sea-green eyes devouring the loveliness of that girl tonight instead of those cold, black evil eyes of Sir Henry Mortimer Draker's, the man her snobbish mother, Lady Moresby, wants her to marry.

Southampton, England

Southampton is the largest city in the county of Hampshire on the south coast of England and is situated 75 miles southwest of London and 19 miles northwest of Portsmouth.

3
REVELATIONS

Captain Beasley faced Edith at the table and true to Arabella's prophecy, he sat gazing at her, devouring her exquisite loveliness in frank admiration.

Subsequently, a thought flashed through his mind. The glow in his eyes faded as he cast them upon his plate before him. The gentle old lady reminded him that he was not eating and asked him what was troubling him. He smiled at her, then at Edith, and murmured, "I think, ladies, that the time has come to enlighten you. I came to Grimsby for a purpose. To fit out a schooner and hunt for the man who hanged my father to the yardarm of his ship and hung him to the gaff of my schooner."

He paused as he noted the look of horror in the girl's eyes, but he went on to tell them that one day when he returned from the banks of Newfoundland loaded down with cod and stepped ashore on the main street of Gloucester, Massachusetts, he was brought up with a jerk by one of his neighbor's son's yelling, 'Captain Beasley, your mother is dead and buried.' From that day on he had carried the burden of sorrows in his heart. From then on, Judson Beasley's story poured forth torrentially, his listeners spellbound as much by the intensity of the man as by the derring-do of his story.

His mother had told him when a boy of how, at home in Portsmouth, England where she was born, she had met and fallen in love with his father. How he had fought with a young lieutenant of the Royal Navy, who had annoyed her with his attentions. And that, shortly after they were married and received the parental blessings of

9

her parents, her father being a wealthy ship owner, they had sailed away aboard his father's ship, a barque, bound for the States where he was born a year later.

His father had carried along with him a letter that was delivered to him the night they sailed from Portsmouth from the lieutenant who swore that he would hunt him down and hang him from the yardarm of his ship.

They had moved from Boston to Gloucester when he was a boy, and later, much against his mother's wish, Judson subsequently went to sea and rose to be captain of a cod fisher.

The death of his mother had ended his life there as a fisherman. He discovered letters in his mother's desk revealing to him that the young lieutenant had resigned from the navy and had become one of the most blood-thirsty piratical-slavers on the middle passage and had subsequently met the barque, "Fanny Rawlings" that his father had named after his mother, and had destroyed her and hanged his father to the yardarm of his ship. But Judson was amazed to discover that his father had been a slave-trader also, like the lieutenant who had sent that cruel letter to his dear mother, telling her he had hanged his father.

After visiting the grave of his mother, he subsequently disposed of his home that he had loved so dearly and left for Boston, vowing that he would never rest until he had avenged his father's death.

With that thought in mind, he had shipped as second mate on a barque called the "Nancy Belle," bound round the Cape of Good Hope to Calcutta. He never reached his destination, however.

The men were kept at the pumps day and night. The barque having sprung a bad leak when west of the Maderia Islands. But Captain Trowbridge, a resident of Bath, Maine, kept on, hoping to reach Cape Town, South Africa.

The men mutinied that day. They insisted that the Captain put in to Funchal. He resisted, with the help of his officers, steward, sailmaker, carpenter, and bosun and got the best of the mutiny. When off Ascension Island, the barque foundered and went to the bottom.

What became of the rest of the crew he never learned. He and some of the men drifted around in one of the boats for several days. They were starving. One of the men went mad and stabbed his shipmate who sat on the throat of the boat in front of him. In the melee that followed, the boat capsized. Jud managed to cling to the keel of it with the steward, but a few hours later, the steward, quite exhausted, let go his hold and sank beneath the waves.

Jud held on grimly; he would not die. He must live to hunt down the man who had killed his father and broken the loving heart of his dear mother.

Out of the dawn that morning, heading directly for him, came the coasting lugger, "Mary Jane." A half hour later he was picked up and cared for by Captain Manley, a native of Boston, England.

The latter, learning that Jud was a navigator, signed him on as second mate, telling him that was the first time he had ever carried one aboard of her. But when Jud asked where the lugger was bound and was told she was heading in to the Bight of the Niger on the slave coast to pick up a cargo of *Black Ebony,* he decided to desert her there and try and learn of the whereabouts of Captain Mort of the "Spitfire".

When they dropped anchor off the Bight, he saw the blue and emerald mountains in the distance and at their base a dense blackness that Captain Bob Manley told him was a forest of jungles and swamps that extended almost to the coast. When he went ashore, he discovered that the cargo of Black Ebony that awaited the lugger was nothing less than a hundred blacks and twenty or thirty of their women who were to be taken to Walfish Bay, southwest Africa, and transported from there across the country to the mines.

Subsequently, the slaves were taken out to the lugger aboard of long-prowed proas (native boats) and chained below decks. But Jud could see the fallacy of trying to desert in that part of the country. He determined to leave her at her port of destination and make his way south to Cape Town and take a steamer for Southampton, England. Later, to fit out a schooner and man her with a crew of naval reserve men and return to the slave coast and do some investigating ashore; for he had discovered while ashore there the remains of the piratical slave ship "Spitfire". While there he had learned that the wreck was stripped of her timbers to build an addition to the castle on the hill that was the home of the lord of that hellish domain.

That night the lugger had sailed away just as the sun was setting in the west. A haze had swept the Gulf of Guinea, but they had not gone far when Captain Manley hove to. A three-masted schooner hove to and signaled her. Jud could not read those signals. They were secret codes. He gazed long and earnestly at her then discovered a fishing smack or coaster hove to a little beyond.

Captain Manley grouched as he lowered his signals and told Jud to stand by to take the painter of the man who was boarding the lugger. A half hour later, a big fat lubber, he said was Portuguese named Bloody Pedro, boarded the lugger with a grin on his face that was disfigured by a scar that reached from brow to chin.

He had barely stepped aboard when he spoke to the men for'ard who seized Jud and disarmed him. Captain Manley had objected, when Pedro told him he was from then on in command of the lugger, "Mary Jane." Five minutes later, Captain Manley and his first mate, Tom Buckley, lay on the deck gasping out their life's blood.

Pedro ordered the men to carry them below. He had called the men by name. He had sailed with every one of them as bosun aboard the "Spitfire" in the days gone by.

Judson Beasley was released and told to go on the look-out and stay there; that if he went aft without orders, Pedro would cut his throat and feed him to the sharks. Jud went. There was nothing he could do about it.

Bloody Pedro had called his men aft and they were handed a pint of rum each, then told to go below, as he and the mate, Judson Beasley, could handle the lugger until eight bells—midnight. As the men went for'ard, he heard the steward yelling his objection to drinking his portion of the rum and it was forced down his throat at the point of a knife in the hands of Bloody Pedro.

Before midnight, the howls of the blacks below decks startled Jud. He glanced aft and saw through the haze that Pedro had left the wheel. He figured Pedro had gone below and got drunk, for the wheel was placed in a becket, as there was not enough wind to keep steering way on the lugger.

Dropping to the deck, Jud stood by the hatch gratings that were fastened down with iron bands and heard the swish of water below decks. He then glanced over the side of the lugger and saw she was sinking fast—going down by the stern. He went below into the fo'c'sle to call the men and found that every man was dead. Bloody Pedro had poisoned the rum. He ran up on deck and thought of going aft to the cabin, but changed his mind. He cut adrift a spar that was lashed alongside the rail and cast it overboard. The next moment, he followed it and clung to it and watched, with gleaming eyes, the lugger go down to the bottom of the gulf with its stinking cargo and crew, and he had no doubt at the time that the bloody murderer, Pedro, had gone down with her.

Drifting seaward with the out-going tide, clinging to the spar, still with the desire to live, he was picked up more dead that alive by a steamer called the "Good Hope" bound from Cape Town to Southampton, England.

Before leaving London, he went to the Fenchchurch Street shipping office and there met up with a former captain of the schooner "Jenny", Jim Barkley by name, who had told him that he had had trouble with the bully of the Barstow fleet in Grimsby and figured he had left him for dead. He had cleared out and was then trying to get a berth as mate on some out-going merchant ship.

Jud gazed at Edith then at the old lady. Smiling, he told them that was a great adventure—and that meeting up with Jim Barkley had inspired him to come to the port of Grimsby and….."

"A great adventure and a most unpleasant one," Edith interrupted, as they rose from the table and proceeded to the parlor, where the Belle of Grimsby became seated at the piano.

Her curiosity satisfied, and likewise that of the old lady, her long, slender fingers glided over the keys. For a half hour, while Mrs. Thornton sat smiling and watching the young couple, Judson Beasley stood by Edith's side entranced, listening to her sweet soprano voice that made a harp of his breast and made him forget all that had gone on before.

Glancing at the clock and noting that it was her grandmother's bedtime, she rose from her seat, her face somehow transfigured by some inner glow, and handed Captain Beasley his cap, as he remarked, "You make me forget all my misery of the past, Edith."

"That is my wish, Jud. I want you to forget, likewise, all thoughts of revenge."

He nodded, wished the old lady good night and followed Edith to the door. Suddenly, she stood on her toes and kissed him. Jud was speechless. With glowing eyes, he left her and shortly after entered the home of the Jenson's, who had gone to bed. He went to his room muttering, "The darling! She gave me a little lip-salve to keep my heart warm until we meet again."

4
DO YOU LOVE HIM

The following morning the long wharf was lined up with buyers of fish from cities near and far. The Barstow fleet had taken on stores and made preparations for their departure with the turn of the tide. The mate of the "Jenny", Victor Jenson, has left the house an hour or more before Captain Beasley tumbled out of bed to get things shipshape before Jud boarded her.

Beasley dressed hurriedly and gulped down his breakfast as Mrs. Jenson told him where she would leave the key as she was going over to her daughter's to spend the day with her and old Lady Barstow at the big house on the hill.

Subsequently, Jud kissed the old lady goodbye and rushed out of the house along the road to the Thornton residence. The door opened wide to receive him before he could knock. Edith ushered him into the parlor, telling him that she had been watching for him to pass. As they became seated, she placed a finger upon her lips, telling him that her Grandma was ill in bed that morning and that they must not make a noise, that she had to postpone her return to London for a few days longer, that her mother had become impatient with her for remaining away from Oak Lodge so long, but that she would not leave Grandma Thornton as long as she remained in bed.

"I regret to hear she had to take to her bed again, Edith, but I am glad you will remain in Grimsby. Sounds selfish, I guess, but I mean just that," he said, a bit gruffly.

She nodded, then chatted away for a half hour, telling him that Sir Henry Mortimer Draker had written her that, while his schooner, the

14

"Angel Girl" was being overhauled, he and her mother and the Countess Catherine du Bois, Sir Richard Tracy, the betrothed of his niece, Margaret Melville, his sister's only child, were leaving in a couple of days for Keswick to go over his estate and see what he could do there for the benefit and comfort of his tenants. From there, they would leave for Birmingham, England to inspect another of the many orphanages he had built in various parts of the country.

She then went on to tell Jud what a wonderful man he was, that his greatest happiness in life seemed to be that of doing everything within his power for the benefit of the poor, donating with lavish hand to various institutions of the country, and that his wealth seemed to be inexhaustible.

Then she laughed, and told him, "He has proposed to me more than a dozen times, Jud, ever since mother and I met him in Paris more than a year ago. The last time," she said, glancing at Jud with an enigmatic smile upon her sweet face, "I slapped his face for him."

"You did?"

"I did so, good and hard, Jud. I wish you could have seen those black eyes of his at that moment."

She then went on to tell him that Sir Henry had returned from one of his trips to the Gulf of Guinea just before she left for Grimsby to visit her grandmother. Her mother, Lady Moresby, the widow of Sir Henry Moresby, had given a dinner to the elite of society in honor of her dear, dear friend Sir Henry Mortimer Draker. She had married shortly after she returned to the stage in London after the death of her fisherman husband, Tom Martin, one of the captain's of the fleet then owned by her grandfather. While the guests were playing for high stakes in the drawing room, she had wondered into the music room and was seated at the piano singing and playing, when she suddenly felt that someone was standing behind her.

Again Edith laughed softly, then told Jud that she was about to get up when Sir Henry proposed to her, clasped her in his arms and kissed her. She had wrenched free from his embrace and slapped his face. He had stood a moment staring at her out of his devilish black eyes, then he had told her she was a little vixen, not the "Angel Girl" he thought her. He had named his schooner "Angel Girl" in her honor.

Jud sat listening attentively, smiling and frowning at times. He wondered what business took Sir Henry to the Gulf of Guinea as Edith went on.

She had told Sir Henry to change the name of the schooner to the "Vixen" and he had blurted, "The Devil!" She had assured him that would be better still; then, turning on her heels, she had flounced away from him and ran up the great staircase to her boudoir, but paused on the landing as she heard Sir Richard Tracy telling his friend that he was a fool where ladies were concerned and he did not know how to handle them.

Sir Henry had remarked, "'Pon my soul, Dick, you amuse me. Have some sense! Women are but pretty playthings."

"And you, you son of a pirate, sicken me!" Sir Richard had blazed at him, a steely glitter in his grey eyes.

Edith said that Sir Henry had called his friend a damn fool. Had he been sensible and taken his advice, he could have returned to England a very rich man. When he married his niece Margaret, he would expect his sister, Lady Melville, to provide for them both ever after.

The two friends came near to blows that night, Edith said, as Jud glanced at his watch, then into the lovely eyes of the girl, who told him that Sir Henry had informed Sir Richard Tracy that he was adding to his great wealth day by day on the west coast of Africa, but that he contemplated retiring from business if Edith consented to become his wife. He had intimated with a devilish laugh upon his lips, it was quite possible that she would be so before he left for the Gulf of Guinea again.

Sir Richard had laughed at him and called him an egotistical prig; then asked him how he was adding to his wealth. Sir Henry informed him that he traded in gold and ivory and sometimes in "Black Ebony" on the slave coast. At that moment Jud sat up and frowned, but whatever was his thoughts he kept silent.

Edith told him that Sir Richard said he would not be a damned bit surprised to learn that he was trading in blacks likewise. Then asked what had become of his father, Sir Henry Mortimer Draker senior. The man who, long years before, had resigned from the navy and disappeared from human kind. Sir Henry informed his friend that his father had died of the sleeping sickness in the jungles of Africa, to which Sir Richard laughingly suggested, you mean on the Middle Passage, don't you?

At that moment Lady Moresby had entered the drawing room and Edith tiptoed to her room, where she sat waiting for her friend

Margaret Melville, as the girl had hinted she wanted to talk of her coming marriage to Sir Richard Tracy, the publisher of the local paper.

Subsequently, she heard footsteps upon the stairs. A moment or so later, Lady Moresby entered her room frowning and began to chide Edith for her actions that night in the drawing room, asking her if she had no respect for her guest.

Edith had told her that Sir Henry had no respect for her and that if she expected her to sell her soul and body to "her friend the devil" she would return to the stage or back to Grimsby where she was born and never return to Oak Lodge again.

Her mother had intimated that she would be marrying a smelly fisherman and would regret it to her dying day. Edith had countered and told her that would be perfectly natural for her to do so inasmuch as she and her grandmother had done so. She had told her daughter Edith, quite frequently, that never again could she love anyone as she had her beloved Tom Martin, who had lost his life up in the North Sea shortly after they were married.

Lady Moresby had sobbingly, then snobbishly retorted that Edith was not the daughter of a smelly fisherman—that her father was a baronet.

Jud glanced at his watch. He rose from his seat then blurted, "I must be going, Edith. Tell me, do you love him? Sir Henry, I mean."

"That remains to be seen, Jud."

"Will you marry me?" he asked, as a nurse she had called arrived at the house. When she had gone upstairs, Edith said, "I'm coming down on the wharf, Jud, to see the fleet heading out."

"You will give me your answer before I leave port?" he asked.

"Yes, Jud, dear," she replied simply as she heard her grandmother calling her. The next moment she kissed him and left him standing on the porch, his eyes gleaming like emeralds.

He hurried back to the cottage and changed into his fishy clothes, then locked the door and made his way back to the wharf with thoughts sacred and profound. But the smile vanished from his face when he thought of what Edith had told him about the noble Sir Henry Mortimer Draker.

"I wonder," he mused, "if there could be any connection between Sir Henry and that bloody, piratical slaver, Black Mort of the "Spitfire?""

Frowning repeatedly, he suddenly blurted, "To hell with them! What more could man wish for than to possess so sweet and charming a girl as the Belle of Grimsby for his wife? When that happy day dawns, dear God, help me forget the sorrows of the past and wipe out of my heart all thoughts of revenge."

The next moment, as he approached the schooner "Jenny", he stopped in his tracks spellbound. Then, as he raced on down the wharf he gritted, "By God, I'll kill that damn lubber!"

5
BULLY BOYD IS LICKED

While Jud was changing clothes, Edith had seen her grandmother and told the nurse that she wanted her to nurse her grandmother nights as she herself could attend to her wants during the daytime; but would she mind staying with her for an hour while she went down to the wharf to see the fleet heading out of the Humber. Grandma Thornton smiled, and assured her she should do so, that she wanted her to see her future husband off on his last trip before she became the wife of Captain Judson Beasley. Edith had blushed then kissed her and went to her room where she snatched up a navy blue cape and threw it around her shoulders and shortly after left the house.

She had arrived there ten minutes before Captain Beasley and was standing on the edge of the wharf conversing with the mate, Victor Jenson, who was on the after deck standing by waiting for his friend, the captain, when suddenly, along the fish wharf came the giant form of Captain Robert Boyd with a sarcastic grin on his face.

Jud had walked swiftly up to them, almost on the run, as Boyd had placed a big hand upon the shoulder of Edith and bent toward her, apparently with the intention of kissing her, Jud thought.

With blazing eyes he caught the giant by the collar, swung him around and landed a terrific blow upon the man's jaw that bowled him over the edge of the wharf.

"Throw that lubber a line, Victor!" Jud yelled as he stood watching the man floundering around yelling for help.

Broad grins spread over the faces of the hardy fishermen aboard the "Jenny." Not one of them had any use for Captain Boyd, known to all as the bully of the fleet. They thought of the wallop they got from Jim Barkley from an iron belaying pin that nearly killed him when he went aboard Captain Barkley's ship and beat him up. They figured that blow from the fist of their captain, the Yankee bean-eater from Boston would settle him for all time to come. Not so, however, for when Boyd was helped aboard, he went back on the wharf and faced Jud.

"What in hell did you mean by that, you damned Yankee son-of-a-sea-cook?" he blazed.

"Another word out of you, Boyd, and I'll ram the words down your throat!" Jud roared. "What right had you to insult the Belle of Grimsby, my affianced bride?"

"I did not. I was about to whisper that I would be best man at her wedding upon our return to Grimsby."

"You know damn well that's a lie, that no other than Victor or Black Jack Barstow could have that honor," Beasley told him pointedly.

"Liar, am I – you damn Yankee! Black Jack will be the groom and not you. Damn you, I'll crush the life out of ......"

Before he could finish, Jud landed a vicious right to the jaw. The giant blonde came near to toppling over the edge of the wharf again. He rose to his feet and rushed at Jud with the intention of getting his muscular arms around him and cracking his ribs with his brute strength, when Beasley side-stepped quickly and sent in a left hook and another right to the man's face. Blood squirted from nose and mouth.

"Come on, you big chunk of beef!" roared Jud. "I'm going to send you aboard the "Grimsby Girl" with your eyes closed and have my mate, your brother-in-law, put you to bed."

"That last smack hit you right on the bloomin' nose, you blighter!" yelled one of the men aboard the "Jenny". "Ten quids to one, mates, that our Yankee skipper licks the bully of the Barstow fleet," he said, with a board grin on his be-whiskered face. But there were no takers from the rest of the crew who was watching the fray amusedly as men from other boats surged around them.

"Jud can handle him mates," Victor remarked. "By God, I didn't know he could use his fists like that! Bully Boyd is crazy for punishment," he said as Jud bowled him over again on his back with another straight right to the jaw.

"Get aboard the "Grimsby Girl" and head out, damn you!"

"To hell with you; you ain't admiral—yet!" Bully Boyd raged as he slunk away, wiping the blood from his nose and mouth as the men aboard the "Jenny" yelled, "Bully Boyd is licked! The Barstow fleet has no longer a bully in it. Our old captain, Jim Barkley, could not handle the blighter with his fists, but he gave him a crack on the head that sent him to the hospital and our captain to hell knows where."

No one had heard from Jim Barkley from that day. Jud wondered at that moment where he was, then turned on his heel to face the girl, thinking she had stood back on the wharf watching him chastise the bully of the fleet, the husband of the girl Edith loved so dearly, but she had immediately returned home, sobbing bitterly. Jud frowned, as his men roared, "Three hearty cheers for our Yankee skipper," they bawled vociferously, as Jud turned a questioning gaze at Victor then was about to retrace his footsteps when his mate called, "Jud, for God's sake, don't go. The tide is on the ebb. In her present frame of mind she would refuse to see you anyway. We have got to get out of here damn quick."

Captain Beasley nodded then boarded the schooner, frowning darkly. The next moment he laughed and told his mate, "I guess you're right, Vic, that girl is upstairs in her room sobbing her heart out at this moment at my ungentlemanly actions. Victor, when I returned home last night, I wanted to tell you that Edith kissed me, but you were sound asleep. When I wished her goodbye this morning, she did so again. I was...."

"Say, you lubber," Victor chuckled, "What if she did kiss you. Why, she kissed me and Black Jack Barstow a dozen times, when....."

"Clear all!" blazed Jud, frowning at his friend.

"Wait a minute, Jud. Let me explain. You know Edith's mother, Lady Moresby, came on a visit to Grimsby and before she left for London gave birth to the Belle of Grimsby in the Thornton home. Eleven years later, when she came on another visit, Black Jack and I fell in love with the lovely girl. We became pals, the three of us, and she never met us but what she would throw her arms around our necks and kiss us repeatedly, telling us we were her great big brothers. Now, Jud..."

"Hell!" laughed Jud. "You sure had me riled. Has she ever kissed you since she has grown up?"

"Never! I daresay she has long since forgotten all about it. Do you know what she came down on the wharf to tell you?"

Captain Beasley laughed. "I can guess, Victor."

"She came to tell you that she would marry you upon our return from the North Sea."

"Clear all!" yelled Jud, happily.

Dacre Castle, Cumbria

Dacre Castle is located in the county of Cumbria in the northwest of England near the border of Scotland.

6
LADY ULRICA THORNTON MORESBY

When Edith entered the house that morning, she told the nurse that she might retire to her room that Arabella had then prepared for her and she could call her for dinner, then sat conversing with her grandmother, who was resting quietly, until the old lady fell asleep. She had refrained from telling her of Jud's actions on the wharf and that she had not wished him goodbye.

She rose from her chair and went to her room and picked up the long telescope and watched the fleet heading out to sea. She wondered, as she had on other occasions, if she would ever see Jud again.

Her mind was like the weather vane floating from the masthead of the schooner "Jenny" at that moment for it seemed to her that the wind was from all directions of the compass.

She could not imagine why Jud had attacked Captain Boyd for he had not said a word to her other than, "Good Morning, Miss Moresby." Boyd had seen Beasley coming along the wharf and was looking for trouble. He hated the Yankee skipper, for no other reason than that he suspected he would be promoted over his head as admiral of the fleet, having overhead a few remarks made by Black Jack Barstow the night before as Jud and Victor left the office.

Suddenly, she saw the blue pennant rise up to the mast head of the schooner "Jenny." Smiling, she laid aside the telescope and picked up one she had made for herself and waved it repeatedly. She noted the fact that Jud had seen it, he had lowered his pennant and hoisted it again. Three times he dipped it in goodbye to her, but not until the fleet of schooners had rounded Spurn Head Lighthouse and was heading up to the Dogger Banks did she leave the window.

After glancing into her grandmother's room again and seeing she was still sleeping, she returned to her room and sat down at her desk to answer her mother's letter and one from Sir Henry and his niece, Margaret Melville, who had written her informing her that upon their return from Dacre Castle at Keswick and Birmingham, she was going to marry Sir Richard and hoped she would return in time for her wedding.

The two girls together made a beautiful contrast for Margaret, like her mother Lady Melville and her uncle Sir Henry, was of a dark olive complexion with blue-black hair and large, jet black eyes. The girls loved each other dearly and Edith wrote her that she contemplated becoming the wife of a captain of the Barstow fleet in the not far distant future, adding that while she hated fish and the smelly, fishy town of Grimsby, she really believed she would eventually get over her dislike for both with the man she loved. She closed her letter to Margaret, who was about Edith's age, telling her not to breathe one word about what she said to any living soul.

Then she wrote to her mother. She found it hard to do so on this occasion. Therefore it was short and to the point. She said that owning to her grandmother having taken to her bed again—really a very sick woman--she could not possibly return home in time to accompany she and Sir Henry on the trip to Dacre Castle.

Edith knew quite well why her mother had insisted upon her return to Oak Lodge. She knew the plans her mother had made for her—that of marrying her off to Sir Henry, a man twice her age—a man who was about the same age as her mother.

Edith had objected to them always, for she possessed—had inherited, in fact, a stubborn disposition from her father who had died when Edith was but a year old. She was determined to be master of her own soul and body.

Sir Henry Mortimer Draker's wealth, his large estates in England, France, and Italy made not the slightest impression on the girl. His love for little children, his charities, and numerous other benevolent enterprises that he was always interested in touched her gentle heart at times, but she told herself that was not sufficient reason for her to yield herself up, body and soul, to a man she feared and did not love--would never love. He was considered to be the wealthiest man in England; one who aspired to becoming Chancellor of the Exchequer in the not far distant future, he had told Edith frequently, but she was not interested.

She wrote on and on with lips compressed. Subsequently, she picked up her mother's letter again and read it. She frowned. Her mother had suggested that after Sir Richard and Margaret were married, she, Edith, should accompany the newlyweds aboard the schooner "Angel Girl" and spend a vacation in Italy at the Villa Rosa, owned by her dear, dear friend Sir Henry Mortimer Draker.

Edith wrinkled up her lovely nose, threw the letter upon the floor, then stomped on it. A moment later she picked it up and tore it to pieces. She understood the meaning of her mother's suggestions, that she should take a trip to Naples with Sir Henry, the countess, and the newlyweds; but such suggestions had no attractions for her.

She bitterly resented those suggestions from her mother and suggested in her letter that inasmuch as she and Sir Henry were of about the same age, they would make a splendid match. Then she laughed at the very idea.

After finishing her letters, she went out to mail them then returned, glimpsing into her grandmother's room a moment. Later, she sat by her window watching the boats sailing up the Humber toward Hull, listening to the raucous cries of the sea gulls as they whirled around close by and to the wind that had risen into gale-like proportions since the departure of the fleet.

Suddenly she murmured, "Oh, Jud dear, why did you do that? I came down to the wharf after telling grandma that I would marry you upon your return to...."

A rap upon the door stilled her tongue.

The nurse stood at Edith's door telling her that Arabella had announced that dinner was served. Would she please come downstairs while her grandmother was sleeping.

Edith nodded. She dressed hurriedly and went down to the dining room where the nurse, privileged to sit at the table with her, was standing by her chair. Together they sat facing each other, but Edith remained silent. Conflicting emotions troubled her sweet soul. She was thinking of fish, fish, fish as the wife of a smelly fisherman. Edith wrinkling up her nose at the moment the freckle-faced, blue-eyed buxom nurse had glanced up at her brought a smile to Alice Seymour's face. The dinner was delicious. She could not understand the why or wherefore of the disgusted expression upon the face of the lovely lady before her.

But the next time she gazed at Edith she caught her smiling. Her smile was irresistible to men and women alike. The nurse breathed inwardly, "How lovely she is!" Edith had come to the conclusion that Jud was possessed of a jealous devil that morning and such thoughts had brought the smile to her face for she told herself that where there was no love, there was no jealousy either.

Several days later she was seated at the window in her room as was her usual custom, when, Arabella, thinking that Edith was resting and not wishing to disturb her, had pushed a letter under her door. The slight noise attracted Edith's attention. She rose and picked it up, glanced at it, then tore the missive open. It was from her mother dated at Keswick.

What her mother said brought a frown to her face. She had been thinking of fish again. Of her mother's brief happiness with her fisherman husband. She wondered if she, too, would be left a widow, if she married Captain Beasley, by his death up in the North Sea.

She sat at her desk and replied at once. She informed her mother that she could not possibly leave for Keswick as her grandmother was still confined to her bed—worse, if anything, than when she had written last. That she had a special night nurse, while she herself attended the invalid during the day and that not until she was quite well again and downstairs could she think of leaving her. She then closed her letter by telling her mother she was disgusted with the town of Grimsby and the noisome odors of fish that drifted even into her room and that but for her grandmother, she would pack up immediately.

After she had dispatched the letter, she wished she had not mentioned one word about fish or the smelly town of Grimsby.

"I wonder what my mother would have said if I had told her that I contemplated marrying Captain Judson Beasley, a man she had never met. Perhaps she would have said she would disinherit me, if I did so. I love him, but I really can't imagine myself being the wife of a fisherman. Fish, fish fish! For the rest of my life in this fishy town I detest so much."

She ended her musings by wrinkling up her nose.

Lady Moresby, upon receipt of her daughter's letter began to wonder if her own mother's illness was really as bad as depicted by her daughter. She told herself that her daughter might be foolish enough to have consented to become the wife of a fisherman captain she had mentioned in a previous letter; a man no one knew or understood.

She packed up immediately and started for Grimsby and upon her arrival, much to Edith's surprise, entered her mother's room and found the old lady much worse than she had expected to find her.

When the doctor called, he informed Lady Moresby that her mother would never rise from her sick bed; that she was failing fast. Irritated that she had to remain there, she told her daughter to go out and visit her friends. Gladly, Edith responded to her suggestion and, for the first time since Jud's departure, her lovely soprano voice pealed forth in song up at the big house of the Barstows' on the Hill.

Black Jack was surprised and delighted when he returned home to dinner. Mrs. Barstow and Jenny, the old lady's daily companion, had urged her to remain for dinner. After dinner, she played and sang for his special benefit and he rewarded her by having his pair of dappled grays hitched up in the phaeton. With Jenny and Edith, he drove around for a few miles and then left Edith at home. Asked in to meet Edith's mother, Jack shook his head and told her he had to get back to his office that night. The truth was he had no desire to meet the snobbish fisherman's daughter who, due to her sweet voice and loveliness, so much like his daughter when she was her age, had been educated abroad like Edith, and became prima donna. She had been lovely and friendly to her neighbors until she returned to Grimsby again as Lady Ulrica Thornton Moresby. Thereafter, she snubbed all of her old friends with the exception of Black Jacks' mother.

When Edith entered the house, her mother, matronly, but still beautiful with that same pinkish-white complexion that her daughter possessed and her large, blue eyes, a shade darker than Edith's, asked her "Is it true, Edith that you have consented to marry Captain Judson Beasley, a man I have never met. A man you told me was a mystery—a man from the far ends of the earth?"

Mischief brightened Edith's eyes, as she glanced casually at the book she was reading, one that Jud had presented to her a week or so before.

"Mother dear," she intoned sweetly, "if my dear grandmother had asked you that same question when you fell in love with Captain

Thomas Martin, what would have been your answer?" she asked, archly.

Lady Moresby was greatly perturbed at her daughter's question. It brought back memories that nothing but death could efface. She sighed deeply, but refrained from answering Edith.

She rose to her feet and with one tearful glance at Edith glided from the room.

She went upstairs to Grandmother Thornton's room and dropped into a chair—thinking of her brief happiness in the arms of her young lover, the husband of twenty-off years before.

When she left the parlor, Edith became seated and caught up the book her mother had been reading, but she sat staring at the pages and saw only the brooding eyes of the man she loved.

"I daresay I shall become the wife of a smelly fisherman, when Judson returns. My mother objects. My dear old grandma consents to my being so. Now what in the world shall I do about it?" she questioned herself, dreamily.

She laid the book aside, after kissing it, rose to her feet and stared around the parlor before putting out the lights, then glided upstairs to her room murmuring, "I shall follow the dictates of my own heart and that will please my dear old grandma, too," she assured herself that night, as she wondered where Jud was with his schooner "Jenny", plowing through the mountainous waves of the North Sea in the fog that seeped in through her open window.

The North Sea

The **North Sea** is a marginal sea of the Atlantic Ocean located between Great Britain, Scandinavia, Germany, the Netherlands, and Belgium.

7
VICTOR BECOMES ENLIGHTENED

Captain Beasley was very happy that day. Fish, fish, fish! No sooner were the lines overboard than they hauled them in again. He told Victor that in a few more days they would be heading back to Grimsby with the greatest catch of the season. Then the "Jenny" would be laid up for a month or even two or three for repairs.

"While you and the Belle of Grimsby proceed to church—after the banns are in—and declare that you will love, honor, and obey each other forever and ever, amen! Then go on a honeymoon trip to Paris, Berlin, Rome, and, maybe, back to America."

"No question about that, Victor. And, I'm telling you and the world that while on our honeymoon trip, I'll give Edith a pleasant surprise. When she learns that from then on I shall be no longer a smelly fisherman but a country gentleman, able to care for her properly, she cannot help but rejoice. And, her snobbish mother, while she may be disappointed for the time being that her darling Edith did not marry the rich baronet she had picked out for the girl to become Lady Draker of Dacre Castle, she will eventually come to her senses, I'm sure."

"I daresay she will," replied his friend. "But, I just don't get the drift of things. What in the devil did you want to buy the schooner "Jenny" for? Figure on Edith having a trip around the world in her?"

"Hardly that, Victor. That would be tempting fate too much. Too dangerous! I would not risk the precious life of my darling in such manner."

It was then Victor Jenson began to get the drift of things to a certain extent. For Captain Beasley went on, "If Edith refuses to become my bride upon our return to Grimsby again, I shall use the "Jenny" for another purpose; that of having her fitted out with guns and a crew of naval reserve men, all fishermen born, sons of the sea, and set sail for the Gulf of Guinea and the slave coast to hunt down that damned piratical slaver Captain Mort who hanged my father to the yardarm of the "Spitfire", after he killed every man aboard the "Fanny Rawlings," the ship my father owned and commanded and then set fire to her on the Middle Passage."

"I daresay I get the drift of that, Jud. But if Edith becomes your wife, then......."

"Then the schooner "Jenny" becomes the property of my best and dearest friend. His name? Captain Victor Jenson, who resigned his command to sail as mate under a bean-eater from Boston, Massachusetts. Get that, Vic?"

Victor's eyes were large and luminous. He gulped, then mumbled, "I daresay—I daresay, Jud."

"When Black Jack finds my check for five thousand pounds honored, as part payment for the schooner under our feet today—well, I guess he will begin to wonder what it is all about. I guess he thought I was kidding him about the purchase of the schooner "Jenny." I never was more serious in my life, Victor."

He told his friend that upon their arrival in port, he was going to ask Jack for twenty quid. He would be going into town to get some little present or other for Edith before visiting her that night.

"If he hands me the twenty, Victor, without any quibbling about it, I'll hand him a check for the balance and add to it the cost for repairs on the schooner."

"You know why he hesitated to sell her to you—don't you, Jud?"

"No, I don't. I offered him really more than she is worth. Why did he object?"

"He loves the schooner "Jenny" as he has ever loved my sister. He named her after her, you know."

"Why in hell didn't he marry her, then?"

"After his father died and he quit fishing on this same schooner, Jenny hung around his office day after day. She loved him. He told her to go home. She went to the theater with Boyd that night and the following morning the bans were in, and...."

"Hard down! Hard down, Victor!" Jud yelled. A tramp steamer was rushing upon them. Bad as the London fogs may be, they could not compare with that which surrounded the fishing fleet up in the North Sea. The steamer missed cutting the "Jenny" into two by thirty feet. Victor laughed as he whirled the spokes of the wheel. Jud boomed, "A close call, that, Victor. We are lucky to be alive at this moment."

"I daresay, Jud. Had she struck us, not a man aboard the "Jenny" would have lived to see the port of Grimsby again. It would have been just another mystery of the North Sea. No one would have known what had happened to us."

"Righto! The captain of that tramp steamer, a scow-wegian, I think, would not have reported the fact that he had run us down. When we leave port we never know if we shall live to get back home again. That is what we fishermen have to contend with always," Jud told his friend, grimly, as he went below, but he did not stay there long. Sleep, he could not.

"That damn fog gets me! I guess I'll go up on deck and, if trouble comes, my pal Victor and I will share it together. Oh, hell! I forgot about that letter Black Jack handed to me the night of our arrival in port. Wonder who it could be from?" he mused.

He searched through his pockets and found it, tore it open and was about to read it when the long, drawn out haunting noise of fog horns and the screaming siren of a steamer brought him up with a jerk, "Another damn tramp!" he grouched.

Victor grinned as Jud faced him. "It's a hell of a life we fishermen lead, Jud. But for my folks, when I left school, I think I should have become a slave-trader on the Middle Passage. We get a hell of a lot of hard work on this job, danger of being cut into two by them tramp steamers, like that one that loomed up like a giant demon from hell on our port beam now, but damn little excitement otherwise."

Jud nodded. When the steamer passed within fifty feet of the "Jenny," leaving her shaking her skirts (sails) in disgust, Jud remarked, "This letter that Black Jack gave me, Victor, I had quite forgotten until a few minute ago. It is from Jim Barkley, who commanded this schooner. I had wondered how he had made out, but what he tells me is interesting. Said that after I left him in Limehouse, a big fat Scotchman came ashore looking for a second mate so he shipped along with him on a three-masted schooner called the "Angel Girl," commanded by Captain Henry, but of all hellions he had ever come in contact with the lubbers for'ard were that."

"Interesting, Jud. If he knew that he had not killed my brother-in-law, he might have returned to Grimsby. I sure did like Jim. Kind of a nervous fellow, but a damn good navigator."

"It is more interesting to me, Victor. He says that all they ever do is take trips to Naples, Italy and fruit and wines, brandy and champagne to Assaba on the Bight of the Niger. Said cargoes were being delivered to the castle on the hill north of the stockades. Now that sets me to thinking deeply, Victor. The Captain Henry he refers to is no other than Sir Henry Mortimer Draker, of Dacre Castle, Keswick."

Victor was about to make some remark or other when he caught sight of one of the fishing schooners on the port beam. Hailing the shadow that loomed up close by, they discovered it was the "Grimsby Girl," commanded by Captain Robert Boyd.

They saw the giant blonde on the after deck cup his hands to his mouth. "Say, Victor," he yelled, "When we get back to Grimsby, I'm going to be best man for Black Jack Barstow. You two lubbers will be on the tail end of it!"

"You're a damn liar!" yelled Beasley, as the "Grimsby Girl" disappeared astern in the fog.

That night, a raging northeaster fell upon them. The outer jib and gaff-sails were taken in and the fore and main double-reefed. The wind howled through the rigging. The schooner "Jenny" went into the trough of the sea, then rose on the crest of a mountainous wave like a cork. Seas boarded her over the bow and rolled aft; but she shook herself free from the smother of it and bucked right into the teeth of the gale.

All through that night with just the forestay sail and double-reefed fore and main, she held her head up to the fury of it. Jud and Victor, lashed to the wheel, with oilskins and sou'westers, laughed at the schooner's antics. They told each other that there was not a boat in the Barstow fleet that could beat the "Jenny" for comfort in such a sea; even while the grey devils of the sea, with their foam-flecked fingers, washed over the little poop deck where they stood laughing and chatting together while they watched the gallant little schooner plunging bow under.

The fishermen for'ard were all under cover. There was nothing more to be done on deck; nothing that her commander could do but turn tail and run before the wind to the Dogger Banks, which he had no intention of doing. She was heading up to the Scandinavian coast, but with the coming of dawn the wind shifted and abated, and little specks of blue burst forth from a leaden sky. Subsequently, it cleared sufficiently for them to see that they were alone on the North Sea. After shaking out the reefs and hoisting the jibs, they headed back to the fishing grounds.

That night, Jud told his friend that his brother-in-law, Captain Robert Boyd hated him for no apparent reason. Victor grinned and informed him that he had probably heard what Black Jack Barstow had said, hinting that he, Jud, would be admiral of the fleet.

"You see, Jud, my sister told me that Boyd was looking forward to being promoted as such. For her sake, I was really hoping that he would become admiral of the fleet. But that lubber is going to get a licking from me someday," he grouched.

"He is that, Vic. I'll tell this cock-eyed world he is—if he ever lays a finger on you or your sister," Jud said, grimly, as they set about getting ready to take in a few more tons of fish.

Subsequently, the little schooner, loaded down with fish—cod and haddock—headed back to Grimsby with the rest of the fleet trailing behind her. The "Grimsby Girl" strove to catch up with the "Jenny" and beat her into port, but neither boat of the fleet had ever succeeded.

When the Barstow fleet headed into port led by the schooner "Jenny," Jud had run up his pennant as usual, but there was no answering signal from Edith. He stood frowning, glancing through his binoculars as Victor said that Edith was probably in her grandmother's room at the moment; could not possibly know they were returning on that day.

Jud lowered his glasses as Victor hauled down the pennant. "I guess you're right, Victor," Jud admitted as they were tying up at the long wharf.

Later, when they entered Black Jack's office and saw the deep frown on his face, they wondered what had happened.

"You found my check okay? What's troubling you?"

"I did, Jud. It was honored at the bank," Black Jack informed him, still frowning

"Loan me twenty quid, Jack. Gold or bank notes. I want to run into town to get a little present for the Belle of Grimsby before I call on her this evening," Jud said.

"I haven't got the cash or notes down here, Jud. I'll get it for you when I go up to the house and call at the Jensons' tonight. You are not leaving port again you know, as the "Jenny" is to be overhauled. Victor can take command of the "Porpoise."

Victor nodded. Jud grinned and said, "Maybe."

They left the office and subsequently stood aghast in front of the Thornton residence. TO LET and FOR SALE signs were in both windows. They went home, Jud shaking his head, his sea-green eyes gloom ridden.

"What happened at the Thornton residence, Mrs. Jenson?" asked Captain Beasley.

"Grandma Thornton died, Jud. After the funeral, Lady Moresby, who arrived shortly after your departure and her daughter Edith packed up and returned to Oak Lodge."

Jenny, the wife of Captain Robert Boyd entered and Jud gazed at her sweet face and asked, "Didn't Edith leave a note with you for me, Jenny?"

"No, Jud. I was with old lady Barstow when they left for London. I daresay her mother hustled her off as quickly as possible, but I am quite sure she will write you—when she has recovered from her great sorrow. Edith was heartbroken, Jud. She loved the old lady so dearly, you know."

"I know she did, Jenny. As for her writing me, I doubt it!" Jud blazed.

With gloom in his eyes, he thanked mother and daughter then turned to his friend, "Let's lope, Vic!" he said, as he left the house.

"Whereaway, Jud?"

"Over to the Fishermen's Rest where we can talk and guzzle," Beasley told him.

8
DRUNK AS A LORD

Captain Robert Boyd had stopped at the Fishermen's Rest after leaving his schooner, which was nothing unusual; he seldom went home sober after a trip up to the North Sea. He was three sheets in the wind, two-thirds drunk, or, apparently so, when Jud and Victor rolled in and called to the buxom barmaid to bring them a quart of half and half as Boyd glared at Captain Beasley, who deigned not to notice him.

The giant lurched over to the table where the two friends sat. Jud was about to tell him to sheer off when Captain Boyd spouted, "Beasley, I bear you no ill-will. You licked me good and fair. You—you are the—only man—in Grimsby that could do it. I want to tell you that I was sorry—that I had no intention whatever of kissing Edith. I was about to tell her that you were behind us," he said, contritely.

"I see," grunted Beasley. Forget it! Have a drink on me," he invited, generously.

"Had enough, admiral," he said, sarcastically, scowling at Victor. "Got to get home to my Jenny."

"You better, and, by God, if you beat her up this trip, I'll send you clean plumb into hell. Don't forget that, Bob. This is my last warning to you," his brother-on-law told him.

"Furthermore," added Judson, glaring up at Boyd, "if her brother don't do it, you can bet your bottom dollar that if I hear of you beating that girl I'll step right in and give you the worst damn licking you ever had in your life. I was only playing with you down on the wharf there," he laughed. "Now get out!" he said, rising from his seat with fists clenched.

Boyd turned on his heels and lumbered to the door. There, he turned and faced them, glaring at Victor. "Got a Yankee prize-fighter to back you up, ain't you. Well, that won't do you any good. Some day, I'm going to break you into two pieces."

"Get home and stay home with your dear little wife," warned Captain Beasley, as he gritted his teeth and made for Boyd. The latter made his exit quickly. Outside he just straightened up. He was not drunk.

Captain Beasley and Victor left the pub an hour later. They were drunk. They had intended going home; in the condition they were they lost all sense of direction. They were lost in the fog. They wandered along the wharf and subsequently fetched up at the "Porpoise," which, along with the "Spurn Head" was one of the worst in Grimsby. Both were patronized chiefly by the riff-raff of all nations, men of the merchant marine.

In the meantime, Captain Boyd had not returned home. He was out looking for trouble again. He had hung around the wharf watching for the two men to leave the public house. He told himself that before he went home he would give both lubbers a licking—one they would never forget.

When he saw them leave the pub, he watched them head off in the direction of the "Porpoise." He was about to follow them when he saw one of his own men trailing along behind them and wondered what he was after; probably, he thought, waiting for a chance to rob them. He grinned evilly and the next moment back up behind the corner of a warehouse. A shadow had loomed up in the fog. He watched the man pass by.

It was twenty minutes later when he stood at the entrance of the pub. There he saw Victor and Beasley leaning on the bar singing a fisherman's song. He entered and walked up to them, caught them by the arm and said he was taking them home. Victor wrenched free and struck Boyd on the jaw. The next moment the two were struggling around the barroom, knocking over tables and chairs. He was beating up Victor when Jud caught Boyd by the arm and gave it a twist that made the giant howl; then Jud landed a blow on the big nose of Boyd, tumbling him over, but did not hurt him much other than to start his nose bleeding. There was not much force behind the blow, as he had caught hold of Jud at the time. Boyd went out grinning, "A hell of a way to treat a man who came down here to do you two lubbers a good turn. To hell with you both! When you are sober, Victor, I'll lick hell out of you—before you set sail for the North Sea again."

Victor staggered after him. Jud barked at him then pulled him back to the bar. The giant was followed by one of his men who hated him like poison. He stood watching him as he disappeared in the fog while shaking his fist at him and muttered, "I see you do it, you bleeding sod!"

The latter, Ted Parker, who had been manhandled by Captain Boyd aboard the "Grimsby Girl" on the first trip out when the giant blond took command of her went back into the pub and sat watching the two friends.

When Captain Boyd returned home, he went to bed wiping the blood from his nose, telling his wife who had sat up waiting for him, as was her usual custom, that he had tried to persuade Jud and Victor to return home but that they had both set upon him

"I daresay that you tried to bully them and got a licking for it. I heard how he whipped you in a fair fight on the wharf. Captain Beasley is a man—all man! Edith told me about it the day after. I do not doubt but what you had it coming to you. You were always jealous of my brother, you big, blustering brute! Tell me, what have you got against them two men—especially Captain Beasley—the man who saved my brother's life up in the North Sea at the risk of his own when he was washed overboard? Answer me, you big drunken brute," she fumed at him.

He rose from the bed and hit her in the face with the open palm of his hand, the blow sent Jenny backward over a chair. "Now shut up, blast you, and come to bed!" he blazed.

Sobbing, she rose to her feet and left the room. She put on her cloak and left the house, a small brick cottage that they rented from the Barstows' on the hill above and went over to her mother's house.

Her mother, with a candle in her hand, opened the door to admit her, thinking that it was Jud and Victor arriving home, until she saw her sobbing daughter who asked, "Are they home yet, mother?"

"No, child," she said sadly. "What has happened? Has that big brute of a husband of yours been beating you again?"

"I fell over a chair, mother. It is nothing. But I am so worried about my brother and his friend, Captain Beasley."

Mrs. Jenson then informed her that Black Jack Barstow had called shortly after dinner to see Jud; that he had some money for him. "I think he said twenty pounds in bank notes. I asked him to leave it with me, but he said he wanted to hand it to him personally, as he had promised," she told Jenny.

Thereafter, mother and daughter went to bed. Jenny sobbing her heart out on her mother's ample breast, telling her she was never, never going back to Captain Boyd again. That she could not stand any more of his drunkenness or brutality.

"Your marriage to Boyd, my child, has embittered the life of Black Jack Barstow. His mother told me that he had loved you devotedly and would never, as long as he lived, care for any other woman. It is a pity, Jenny, that you acted so foolish that night, for, I am quite sure you would have been a very happy...."

"Yes, mother," she interrupted, "please don't say anymore about it. I have tried to be a good wife to Bob, but he handles me like a brute beast and I can't go on," she concluded.

What Ted Parker had seen Captain Boyd do during the scrimmage at the Porpoise he kept to himself. He believed if he tattled about it his captain would see to it up in the North Sea that he would never have a chance to do it again. He loafed around, following Victor and Beasley, curiously, while keeping in the background and, strange to say, sober, which was something unusual for him.

He followed them from the Porpoise to the Spurn Head Tavern, a half mile along the wharfs. Jud and Victor stood there at the bar singing. For the time being, they had forgotten what had upset both men completely: Edith's departure from Grimsby without leaving one word for Captain Beasley.

They were drowning their sorrows, having talked over their plans for the future, before they lost all sense of wit. Suddenly, Jud stuck his hand in his pocket and brought out a few, crisp bank notes. He stared at them unsteadily, then laughed, "I guess, Vic, that...we...can hit....her...up...again," he said brokenly.

"I dare – say, Jud," Victor chuckled, foolishly, as he saw Jud throw one of the notes down on the bar and call all hands to drink to his health, declared that when the sun rose above the mountains again he would be hanging to the yardarm of his ship the man who had killed his father. Victor nodded, and then some of the men roared, "The skipper be thinking of Captain Boyd, mates." The rest of them, in drunken stupor, yelled, "Fill'em up, Polly. Three cheers for Captain Beasley who licked the bully of the fleet and is going to hang him from the fore-peek of the "Jenny" on our next trip out in the North Sea."

Ted Parker stood beside Jud watching Polly make change for the note Jud had so carelessly thrown upon the bar.

"I be not drunk, Polly. I see ye do it," he grimaced foolishly, gazing at her craftily out of his bloodshot, bleary blue eyes as he wiped his mouth on the sleeve of his pea jacket.

"You blasted shrimp!" she fumed at him, as she handed Jud the balance of his change that she had held back. Jud taking no notice whatever of what they were squabbling about, picked up the change then handed Polly a half sovereign.

"That is the second time Captain Beasley gave me that rhino," she said, glaring at Ted Parker. "If you make any more insinuations like that I'll have my father throw you out into the gutter!"

Ted drew back from the bar and with glass in hand sat at one of the tables sipping his pint of half and half, but kept his eyes upon Captain Beasley and his friend.

When Black Jack Barstow left Mrs. Jenson that night in search of his two friends, he had not the slightest reason to expect to find them in any public house in Grimsby. He knew that both men were the soberest of the fleet and that they never spent their evenings in such places.

Jack had paused at the Thornton home and glared at it through the fog. He shook his head sadly. He wondered what Jud thought of Edith—leaving town without wishing any of her friends goodbye. He sorrowed greatly for his friend Jud, knowing that the Yankee worshipped the girl. He could not understand why, if Edith loved the man, she had left for London without leaving one word for him with his mother, Mrs. Jenson, Jenny, or even Mrs. Bailey, her next door neighbor, the wife of one of the mate's of the fleet.

"I daresay that snobbish mother of hers prevailed upon the Belle of Grimsby to return home and marry that blighter, Draker," he mumbled to himself as he paused in front of the Fishermen's Rest, while on his way to his office. Just at that moment one of the fishermen of the fleet lurched drunkenly out of it.

"Hey, you drunken duffer! Have you seen Captain Beasley and his mate Victor lately?" he asked.

"Aye, I did. Left the pub as drunk as a lord, Captain. Then they went 'ome. I be sober an'....."

Black Jack had no objection to his men taking a drink upon their arrival from the North Sea but he detested a habitual drunkard. He caught the man by the scruff of the neck, turned him around facing the city and gave him a kick.

"Get home to your wife and children, Joe. The next time I run afoul of you and find you drunk, I'll give you the sack," he blazed at the man.

"Jud and Victor drunk? That could never happen! I daresay they went to a theatre," he concluded, as he went on to the wharf, feeling his way in the fog.

He stood by the door leading into his office, searching for the key when a shadowy form rose up behind him and gave Jack a whack on the head that bowled him over on his back.

The watchman, making his rounds, found the owner of the Barstow fleet bleeding with a slight wound on his forehead, his pockets all turned inside out. He blew his whistle and in five minutes two bobbies came running up.

"Drunk as a Lord," one of the policemen said.

"Ye be daft to say so, ye bloody duffer," Jimmy Thompson, the watchman, said. "Any bugger can see that some blighter black-jacked Black Jack Barstow and that robbery was the motive."

The bobbie who had not spoken, said "Righto, Jimmy! You should be in Scotland Yard. Lend a hand and help me get Jack home. He is only stunned." A half hour later they carried him into the house where his mother awaited him.

9
IT'S A BLOOMIN' SHAME

Jack Barstow's mother had sat up waiting for her son. The old lady had expected him to return that evening at 9:00 pm as he had promised her he would, but for the first time in his life he had disappointed her. It pained her deeply. Her large black eyes were moist with tears.

When the police brought him home and she saw blood on his face, she swooned away. Doctor Spalding, whom the police had called on their way to the Barstow residence, had followed immediately and quickly brought her round. With tear-dimmed eyes she asked, "What has happened to my son?"

"The watchman on the wharf found 'im unconscious by 'is orffice, Mrs. Barstow," replied one of the men. "He said as 'ow he found 'im with 'is pockets turned inside hout. But don't you be worrying, we'll get the blighter that did it. But I arsk you, did Black Jack 'ave any money with 'im?"

"He did. Twenty pounds in bank notes but he left that money with Captain Beasley at the home of Mrs. Jenson shortly after 7:00 pm. He said that after doing so he would run over to his office for some papers he had forgotten."

Doctor Spalding, having dressed the wound on Jack's head, had assured his mother that he was in no danger. He told her that he would call again next day and that she should keep him in bed; that he would be up and about in a few days.

"It's a bloomin' shame!" commented Jerry Townsend, as they left the house. "But I don't think anyone 'it Jack Barstow on the 'ead. I still think he was drunk, Bill."

"I don't. Any blighter could see that. I didn't get a smell of rum on his breath."

"I'll get the man who did it," said Bill Barlow, the other policeman, as he sent in a report to headquarters.....

When Black Jack opened his eyes, he gazed around his room and saw his mother seated by his bedside. He wondered what it was all about. His hand went up to his bandaged head. His mind cleared a bit. He remembered his visit to his office on the wharf, but that was the last he could remember.

"How did I get home, mother?" he asked.

She told him, then placed a hand upon his head. "Go to sleep, Jack. I'll tell you more about it in the morning."

"Just got a thundering headache, that's all," he grinned.

After breakfast, which he ate in bed, Jack was telling his mother what had happened. Not finding Jud and victor home, he had come to the conclusion they had gone to a theatre, and..."

Before he could finish a rap came upon the door and to Mrs. Barstow's 'come in' the maid admitted Jenny Boyd.

Gazing tearfully at Jack, she sat by his bedside, his mother's arm about the neck of the girl that she had in the years gone by looked forward to calling daughter. Jenny clasped her hand as her eyes filmed over. A moment later she burst into tears. Her head fell forward upon the bed. Jack's hand passed over her chestnut-brown locks caressingly while his mother soothed, "There, dearie! Please do not carry on so, darling. There is absolutely nothing to worry about. Jack met with a misfortune—an accident last night just before entering his office. While he lay unconscious on the wharf, some footpad went through his pockets."

"But," said Jenny, after a fleeting glance at Jack, "it is whispered around that—that....."

She broke down again with head bent low and remained silent. She couldn't tell them it was whispered around the public houses that her brother and Captain Beasley had waylaid and robbed the owner of the fleet.

"Jenny," said Jack, kindly, "it is all my fault. I just read in the paper that..."

"You believe those statements about my brother and Captain Beasley?"

"No, Jenny. I'd ram the lie down the throat of the man who said it—if I knew who the man was." She nodded and left them.

10
I SEE THE BLIGHTER DO IT

A couple of very sober men in gaol awaited trial. Captain Judson Beasley and Victor were charged with assaulting and robbing Black Jack Barstow.

After Jenny departed, Jack was reading the paper to his mother, then laughed. "Imagine, mother dear, a man who could hand over a check for five thousand pounds waylaying me for so paltry a sum. The idea! Expect two guests for dinner, mother. Doctor Spalding is crazy to think that I'm going to remain in bed for several days just because I got a rap on the head."

He rose and dressed hurriedly, then ordered his carriage, telling his mother he would have his friends out of gaol in a jiffy and that he would bring them home with him And, just as he was leaving the house, Ted Parker came up to him with a grin on his face.

"Captain Barstow, I see the blighter do it with me own eyes; I did for sartin, sir," he said, wiping his mouth on the sleeve of his jacket.

"See what?" barked Black Jack, his black eyes blazing at the drunken lout.

"I see Captain Boyd put them bank notes into Captain Beasley's pocket—when he was wrastlin' with him at the Porpoise," Parker told him.

"Are you sure of that, Ted?"

"I be, Captain. Sartin sure; but if he lives and learns that I told ye, sir, he will be doing for me up in the North Sea," said Parker with a shudder.

"Get in my carriage. I need you. I'll have that duffer arrested. As for sailing under the Barstow colors, he is finished," vowed the owner of the fleet.

"I hope so, Captain. Ye see, he be in the orspittle dying!" Parker exclaimed, grinning at him.

"What happened to him, Ted?"

"He got a knife stuck into him a half dozen times—just before the pub closed. He went into the Spurn Head Tavern and insulted Tom Carney's darter, the barmaid. She refused to serve him at the bar and he called her a name and caught her by the throat and choked her. Then he left, followed by her father and I trailed along behind him. I saw Tom Carney staring in the window of the Porpoise and when I come up to him I said, 'What's up, Tom'? And he said there was no charnce for him to beat up Captain Boyd. He was grinning at the time and knowing him to be a one time heavy-weight champion of England, I had followed him to see Boyd get another licking. I looked in the window and saw a half dozen foreign merchant sailors, all of them raising hell in there. I saw Boyd pick up one of the lubber's and throw him at the rest. They went down in a heap, all but one little dago, who had crept up behind Captain Boyd, jumped on his back and bury his knife into him again and again. Then the sailors all ran out of the pub and went back to their ship, which left port on the ebb tide. I ain't happy about it, am I?" he laughed.

After Boyd hit his wife and she left the house, he was as mad as hell. Five minutes later he left there also and went back to the pubs looking for trouble. He was hunting Beasley and Victor with the intention of manhandling them both. He got what he was looking for and died in his wife's arms that morning as Jud and Victor left gaol with Black Jack Barstow.

He invited both up to the house with him. He wanted to talk matters over with them; with Jud especially. Captain Beasley refused, telling him he had some business to attend to that was pressing indeed, and that he needed Victor's help. Jack insisted they both return and take dinner with him and his mother and Jud replied, "Maybe, Jack! What's on your mind."

When the Jenny is ready for sea, you are admiral of the fleet. Victor takes command of the Grimsby Girl which is now ready to leave on the ebb tide."

Jud laughed, shook hands with Jack, then turned on his heel and followed his friend Victor to the home of the Jensons'.

When Victor returned to the Barstow residence, he told Black Jack in his office that Judson Beasley had left Grimsby for London to call on Edith at Oak Lodge. He handed Jack some papers and a sealed letter, telling him that Jud had said if he failed to contact Edith he would not return to Grimsby for some time—if ever. He would be leaving London in quest of "Her Friend the Devil"—if he was not in port. He wanted to have a quiet talk with him about Captain Mort of the old "Spitfire."

"The Belle of Grimsby! Her departure and silence drove him from Grimsby. I think he was a fool, but if he ever needs us, Victor, I'm telling you that nothing would give me more pleasure than to assist him in every way possible."

"Jack, those are my sentiments, too. What in the devil he made that will for—in my favor—leaving me the Jenny all paid for and twenty thousand pounds, if, as he said, he kicked in, leaving the balance of his estate to my sister amounting to fifty thousand pounds. It has got me all muddled up. In the event he returns to Grimsby with Edith as his wife, he told me the will would be null and void.

Black Jack commented, "He did not pay the balance agreed upon for the purchase of the schooner, Victor."

"You will find that and more added to it in that letter," Victor told him, chuckling inwardly.

Jack tore it open, then gasped, "A check for ten thousand pounds. My God, Victor! Captain Beasley must be daft."

"I daresay. So was I for not going along with him. I wanted to, but he told me that my sister and mother would be needing me and that I was to take command of the "Jenny." After you cash that check, Jack, I want the bill of sale for her. He told me that if he did not return inside of a week or ten days to get the will recorded. If we did not hear from him in a year's time, he would be under the sod or at the bottom of the ocean."

"I have an idea that we shall hear from him again, shortly. A man of Jud's character and caliber don't kick the bucket so easy as that.

"You're right, Jack. What about the Grimsby Girl?"

"Could not wait for you. Forget it! Bailey is in command of her. You can wait for the Jenny and if Jud has not returned by the time she is ready, you go aboard her as admiral of the fleet."

Victor gulped, but remained silent as the coachman-butler announced that dinner was served.

A week after the funeral of Captain Robert Boyd, Jenny, her mother and Victor were seated at the Barstow table. Jack was telling the ladies that he had promoted Victor; that when he left port again; he was in command of the Jenny as admiral of the fleet. However, he did not own a stick of the schooner that he loved so much.

Victor had not mentioned one word to his sister or mother about Judson Beasley having purchased her. His sister, glancing at Black Jack with those wide-open eyes he loved so, asked, "And who might the new owner be, Jack?"

"Captain Judson Beasley. If he doesn't turn up in a year's time, your brother will own her and above the door of my office will be a new sign reading, 'BARSTOW & JENSON COMPANY'," he informed her, smiling.

"I do not understand Captain Beasley," she said, simply.

"Neither do I, but mark ye, Jenny, there was a man I would go to..."

He paused, glanced at Victor, then muttered grimly, "You know where, Victor."

"I daresay, it would be hot enough for me down there, in the Gulf of Guinea," Victor concluded, laughing.

London, England
London is the capital city of England and the United Kingdom
located on the River Thames.

11
LITTLE PIECES OF PAPER

When Captain Beasley arrived in London, he drove to a west end hotel where he secured accommodations. The following morning, after an early breakfast, he called at Sir Richard Tracy's office only to find that he, his wife, and her mother, Lady Melville were sojourning on the continent. Sir Henry had set them ashore at Le Havre, regretting that business of the greatest importance prevented him from taking them to his Villa at Naples, Italy.

The manager of the local paper that was owned and published by Sir Richard had requested the name of his caller and Jud told him, "Well that doesn't count. Just wanted to interview Sir Richard for my paper back in the States. Thanks! Good luck, my friend," he concluded, as he turned quickly on his heels and strode away swiftly to his cab.

On the way back to his hotel, he told himself that it was rather early to call on the Belle of Grimsby at Oak Lodge out on Berkeley Square.

As he entered the lobby and picked up a paper, he sat down musing before glancing at it, telling himself that his trip to the office of the newspaper had probably saved him much unnecessary worry. Then he scanned over the front page of the paper he held in his hand at the face that stared out at him on the front page. It startled him greatly. Above it was the caption, "Prima Donna". Below it, he read:

"Edith Virginia Moresby, the lovely girl pictured above, whose fine soprano voice has thrilled thousands nightly in Paris, Berlin, and Rome and appears at the Drury Lane Theatre tonight as Lucia in "Lucia Di Lammermoor".

She will be remembered in years to come as one whose melodious voice was unequalled only by that of her own lovely mother, Lady Ulrica Thornton Moresby, the widow of Sir Henry Moresby, who, it will be remembered, closed her career on the stage as Queen of Night in "The Magic Flute".

At the conclusion of her engagement, it is said that the young Prima Donna and the Countess Catherine Du Bois will leave for the Villa Rosa at Naples aboard of the schooner-yacht Angel Girl; owned and commanded by Sir Henry Mortimer Draker, the great philanthropist.

It is whispered that Edith Virginia Moresby and Sir Henry will be united in marriage at his villa in Naples and that he is now retiring from business for all time to come. Upon their return to England, the happy bride and groom will make their home at his ancestral estate, Dacre Castle at Keswick."

Jud threw the paper aside and scowled. A moment later he picked it up again and stared at Edith's pictures, then commented, "I understand your silence now, Edith. You have chosen your friend the devil—as you were pleased to call Sir Henry. Fate, that I believe in today, plays a fellow some dirty tricks. Fate, aided by Lady Moresby, has driven you into his arms. It is useless for me to call on you, but, by God! I'll......"

***

That night in an inconspicuous sea, he sat like one entranced in the theatre listening to Edith's lovely voice. The first act finished to thunderous applause. He quickly made his exit from the theatre, called a cab and drove back to his hotel.

He sat in the lobby meditating over the past, the present, and what the future held for him. Again, he picked up the paper and the next moment he cut out the picture of the Belle of Grimsby and the words attached and placed it in his pocket book.

"I never expect to meet you again, Edith, but I'll meet that black devil Draker somewhere, somehow, and.......Well, I'll have a nice quiet talk with him."

He went to his room muttering, "Perhaps, if I had been honest with Edith and told her that the day she became my wife I would retire to some country estate with her and never, never care to wander again, she would have..."

He paused. Frowned. Then, a few moments later muttered, "Oh, hell!"

The following morning he checked out of the hotel, having secured passage the evening before for Funchal, Maderia Islands. That same morning, as he boarded the steamer, Edith asked her mother at the breakfast table, "Mother dear, after I had written a letter to Captain Beasley before we left Grimsby, you suggested that while I packed my trunk you would visit Mrs. Jenson and leave that letter with her for Jud upon his arrival in port. Are you quite sure that you did not forget?"

"Quite sure, my child," she lied, turning aside.

"I cannot understand his silence," the girl sighed.

"I can, my darling. After the disgrace he and Victor brought upon themselves, waylaying and robbing Black Jack Barstow as they did, it is only natural to suppose that some sense of shame and decency prevented him from writing. A letter from him under the circumstances would be an insult."

"There is some mistake, mother. Neither Jud nor Victor is capable of doing what they are accused of. I am going to write Jud in care of Black Jack Barstow," she said, adding, "Jack will see that he gets the letter the moment he returns from the North Sea."

"Very well. Write immediately, my child. Tell him that he will find a welcome here at Oak Lodge and that you......Well," she smiled, "you can tell him what is in your heart upon his arrival here. I am going out to luncheon with Lady Leona Barry and will mail it for you—if you hurry," she suggested, as Edith started upstairs to her boudoir.

Edith wrote rapidly. She told Jud that she had given her mother a letter to leave with Mrs. Jenson for him and that he should visit her at Oak Lodge in London; that while she had read of him and Victor being arrested, etc., she did not believe one word of the charges against them. His silence, she wrote, had made her so very unhappy she had accepted an engagement on the stage that would probably last for three months. Thereafter, she would pack up and return to Grimsby to become his wife for she loved him a thousand times more than she hated fish and the town where she was born.

She assured him of her faith in him; assuring him of her undying love for him always and closed her letter by signing herself, "Your own darling Edith!"

Her mother came downstairs at that moment, paused before her and glanced at the great grandfather's clock that was then chiming eleven and said, "I'm leaving now, darling. If you have not the letter ready you must mail it yourself, dear. I cannot wait," Lady Moresby announced, as Edith sealed her letter and stamped it.

"Here it is, mother. Thank you!" She smiled as she handed the letter to her mother who kissed her and departed, smiling likewise.

Seated in her Victoria behind her liveried footman and coachman, still smiling, she tore open the letter.

Her brows came down. She frowned, "The very idea! How idiotic! I thought my daughter had more sense. Now, if she had written such a letter to my dear, dear friend, Sir Henry, the nobleman, the great, good, generous soul that he is, there would have been some sense to it; but to write such to a smelly fisherman—a man of mystery—a man who is in gaol at this time, is more than I can understand.

"'Your own darling Edith.' That shall never be. There must be some way to prevent them meeting again for after he is released from gaol, he will probably be coming up to London and call at my home. I must remain at home hereafter and see to it that she does not meet him," she concluded, sighing.

Her ample bosom rising and falling with the turbulence of her heart, she tore the letter into small pieces and, with compressed lips, left behind the Victoria a trail of fluttering little pieces of paper that Judson Beasley would have given his very life for, had he known what had been written upon them.

Cape Verde
Cape Verde is an island country spanning an archipelago of 10
islands located in the central Atlantic Ocean.

12
IN QUEST OF THE DEVIL

While Captain Judson Beasley was speeding away to the port of
Funchal where he hoped the Angel Girl might drop anchor in
the roadstead and see Sir Henry come ashore there, the schooner was
beating her way up from the Gulf of Guinea, homeward bound again.

Jud's one consuming desire now was to encounter Draker
anywhere but in London. He believed it possible, after what he had
learned from Edith, that he would learn something from him
concerning the scoundrel who had murdered his father.

The very fact that he was associated with the doings on the slave
coast inspired that belief. He believed also that at the castle on the hill
at a point north of Assaba he would learn the whereabouts of Captain
Mort, and he wanted that ruffian's head above all things else on that
day. He swore that, eventually, by hook or by crook, he would enter
that castle. If he had known a few things more before leaving Grimsby,
that Jim Barkley could have told him, who was at that moment second
mate of the "Angel Girl," he would have remained in Grimsby or
returned there immediately from London and waited until the schooner
Jenny had been overhauled. The Jenny had been manned by a husky
crew of Grimsby fishermen who would have gladly followed him to
hell and back if necessary. He did not, but he was glad he had told his
friend Victor of his intentions if the Belle of Grimsby refused to return
with him as his wife.

It was fated that he was to meet Jim Barkley again on the beach at Funchal. The man who thought he had killed Captain Boyd who had been intimate with his wife on several occasions. The wife who had suddenly left Grimsby when she heard that her lover had been taken to the hospital in dying condition sent there by her husband, fearful of Jim's vengeance upon her also.

When Barkley met Jud Beasley in the shipping office and later went across the road to the Chain & Anchor pub to get a quart of half, he told Jud he was late captain of a schooner belonging to the Barstow fleet at Grimsby. He was in such a damned hurry to get away that he was ready to ship on any old tub that came along, which was the obvious thing for him to do, he thought.

On this trip, heading up to Funchal from the Gulf of Guinea, when about thirty miles due west of Cape Verde, he heard the mate who had signed him on talking with Captain Henry. The mate, Sandy McIntosh, a big, raw-boned Scotchman with small, piggish looking eyes set close together, was sitting on top of the after cabin house smoking his short, black clay pipe telling Captain Henry that Jim Barkley, the second mate, would never go into the jungles back of Assaba with his pet bloodhounds, Belial and Lucifer behind him, thirsting for his blood as the last two second mates did.

"As long as he minds his own business and makes himself scarce going to the break of the poop as he does, when I'm on deck talking to you or the countess, he will never have that pleasure," chuckled Captain Henry.

Sandy nodded as the Captain, who stood at the wheel steering the schooner on that day, went on, "You remember when I went ashore at Funchal, Sandy, a year or more ago, a couple of months or more after Pedro visited us while we were hove to in the gulf that night as the sun was setting?"

"I do, Henry!" grouched Sandy.

"For a man who had cut the throats of nearly a hundred men—before I captured him and his brig when I was mate of the old Spitfire—he died a very peaceful death. Like you, Sandy, he was not born to be hung," he chuckled.

Sandy blazed. "Aye, Captain, but I'm a wee bit supersteetious aboot that."

"'Pon my soul," laughed Captain Henry, "I'm not. I have a feeling that you and I were born to be drowned. Of course….."

Sandy interrupted him. "I'm a wee bit supersteetious aboot that, too. This is my last trip, Henry. Do ye ken that mon?" he asked, as he dropped to the deck and went below to get a drink and fill his pipe while Captain Henry muttered, "His last trip? Well and so it is."

Ten minutes later Sandy came up on deck again and seated himself upon the cabin house facing Captain Henry. He glanced up at the sails and said, "Keep her full, Captain. Ye be shaking hell out of her. What in hell….."

Suddenly the mizzen-boom jibed over and caught Sandy amidships, lifting him over the side into the sea.

"Man overboard! Let go the jib sheets. Lower away the gig, bosun!" roared Captain Henry, as he glanced astern.

Jim Barkley, the second mate, heard Captain Henry yelling and ran up on deck barefooted to take command of the boat, but Captain Henry countermanded the order.

"Useless," he said. "The sharks tore poor old Sandy to pieces before my eyes, Mr. Barkley," he remarked sadly, dropping from one of his gleaming black eyes the monocle that he wore when things pleased him.

"You will, as first mate of the "Angel Girl," Mr. Barkley, enter your report in the log. It was quite an accident. One that is likely to occur at sea at any time. The wind shifted suddenly," he said, as he gave orders to hoist up the jibs again, then called a man aft to the wheel.

"Aye, aye, sir!" Barkley replied, as he went below and wrote in the log as directed, but he wondered while doing so how in hell the boom-guy had got adrift, for when he went below deck to get a snooze he was quite sure it was fastened to the bits with a half hitch.

It was near one bell and Jim, after closing the log, went to his room and dressed and then ran up to the deck, where he saw Captain Henry smoking his bull-dog pipe and laughing. For'ard were two giant Dahomey blacks exercising the bloodhounds that Captain Henry had purchased three years before. Up in the rigging were the watch on deck, out of reach of their fangs.

Captain Henry on the weather-side of the deck called to Barkley and commented, "We may possibly pick up a man on the beach at Funchal to take your place as second mate, Mr. Barkley. I have met many good men there and some I talked with onshore were navigators, others just beachcombers. If you cannot find one, then upon our arrival at Gravesend, you will do so."

"Aye, aye, sir!" replied Barkley, saluting him as Captain Henry went below. A few moments later he came up on deck with the countess whom he, Jim, had always addressed as Mrs. Henry for her morning promenade upon the deck with the master of the schooner.

Three weeks later he dropped anchor in the roadstead at Funchal. Judson Beasley was in one of the largest casino's at the time, but the news of the arrival of the "Angel Girl," spread quickly and on his face was an enigmatic smile as he went down to the beach, watching for a boat to come ashore from her with the man he wanted to meet—face to face. But he was disappointed that night.

The following morning Jud was down on the beach quite early with a half dozen other men who followed the sea; men he had given a handout to since his arrival there, wondering how in the devil they lived and where they slept at night.

He had breakfasted quite early and was waiting anxiously for a boat to be lowered from the Angel Girl bringing Sir Henry ashore. He had learned that the owner of the schooner, after anchoring there, had always come ashore for a few hours before weighing anchor and sailing away north again. On her return, she had stopped there to take fruit and wines aboard.

Imagine Jim Barkley's surprise when he came ashore to see Judson Beasley there. He exclaimed, "Well, Captain Beasley, this is a pleasure! But say, what is the trouble? Is Scotland Yard after me for the murder of Captain Robert Boyd?"

"Murder nothing, Jim. That bully did not croak. But he is dead and buried now. I came here to get in touch with Sir Henry Mortimer Draker, the owner and commander of that ship of yours. Why in hell didn't he come ashore?" he blazed.

"You mean Captain Henry, don't you? I don't know him by any other name."

"That's him, and if I mistake not, Jim, he is connected with the piratical-slaver Captain Mort of the Spitfire. That is why I want to meet him here, instead of in London where he is a power in the land and well beloved by most folks."

"The first mate of the Angel Girl got knocked overboard on the way up from the gulf by the mizzen-boom and—well," he said, grimly, "Captain Henry said it was an accident. You see, it was my watch below and he was at the wheel. Sandy McIntosh, the first mate sat on top of the cabin house and suddenly the boom jibed over and lifted him over the side. Shortly after, he told me I was first mate and that if I could not pick up a navigator to fill my place as second mate ashore here I should do so upon our arrival at Gravesend."

"Do you believe in fate, Jim?"

"I do. Don't you?"

"I do that, Jim. I am a fatalist. I believe everything is cut and dried for us. Sign me on, Jim. Maybe I'll make one round trip with you; then again, maybe I'll leave you upon our arrival in England."

Jud then went on to tell Jim of what had happened back in Grimsby and of his love for the Belle of Grimsby, who had left the port with her mother, Lady Moresby, after the death and burial of Grandma Thornton, ending with, "I came here in quest of the devil, Sir Henry Mortimer Draker. Sign me on as Judson Bennet, Jim, for I have not the least doubt about it that your Captain Henry has heard of Judson Beasley, Captain of the schooner Jenny from Edith's mother."

An hour later, the mate took Beasley aboard the Angel Girl and introduced him to Captain Henry who glared at him out of his monocle for a moment. He let it fall, dangling upon its cord as he asked, "Are you a navigator, Bennet?"

Jud had been taking his measure. He glared back at Captain Henry, but a smile wreathed his pleasant features.

"I am, sir! Late mate of the "Merry Hell" bound round the Cape of Good Hope to Calcutta, general cargo from New York back in the States. An old tub leaking like the devil ever since leaving port. Pumps clogged. Could not keep her afloat to get to port. Foundered and went to the bottom. Picked up by a steamer bound to Cape Town. Set ashore here—not wishing to go there. Lost all my papers and belongings," he concluded, grimly.

Apparently satisfied with Bennet, he commanded, as he was going below decks, "Get under weigh, Mr. Barkley."

"Aye, aye, sir!" replied the mate, as he went for'ard with Beasley, introducing him to the men as the new second mate.

Jud whispered as he gave the order to the men to break out the anchor and cathead her, then stand by to hoist the jibs and lift up the throat and peek of the fore, main, and mizzen sails, "You were right,

Jim. Every one of these lubbers here for'ard were members of some piratical slaver on the Middle Passage[1], I'm sure."

Jim Barkley nodded as he went aft. Jud grinned and muttered, "I guess it will pay me to make a round trip on the Angel Girl and learn what I can there at the slave coast about the late Captain Mort of the Spitfire.

---

[1] The **Middle Passage** was the leg of the Atlantic slave trade that transported people from Africa to North America, South America and the Caribbean. It was called the Middle Passage as the slave trade was a form of Triangular trade; boats left Europe, went to Africa, then to America, and then returned to Europe. http://www.wordiq.com/definition/Middle_Passage

Gravesend, England

Gravesend is a town in northwest Kent, England, on the south bank of the Thames.

13
THE ABDUCTION

On the way up to the channel, Barkley told Beasley that on the last trip down to the Gulf of Guinea, he had gone below, but could not sleep. The countess Catherine Du Bois had been taken ill and that her maid, Lallah, a young Egyptian woman and the mulatto steward had been pattering around the cabin so much they kept him awake. Up on deck he heard the mate, McIntosh, arguing with Captain Henry and he stuck his head out of his port to listen in, knowing they were on the weather-side of the schooner, but all he could catch was that one word, "Spitfire."

Jud grinned at that. "I guess I'm on the right track, Jim. Furthermore, I wouldn't be a bit surprised to learn that his own father was commander of her. I thought of deserting this packet when we reached England, but I have come to the conclusion I should make a round trip on her. Why? Because I firmly believe that he lied when he told Sir Richard Tracy that his father died of the sleeping sickness in the jungles of Africa; that the Lord of that hellish domain at the Bight of the Niger in the castle on the hill is no other than his father or that damned piratical slaver, Captain Mort.

"Let me warn you, Jim. Don't ever forget that my name is Bennet and not Beasley as long as I remain aboard here."

Barkley nodded, walked aft from the break of the poop, glanced aloft at the sails and binocular; gave an order to the helmsman and returned to Jud and whispered, "Here's a tip worth having, Jud. That damn mulatto steward is a spy for Captain Henry and will be listening in on us indefinitely. Watch your step!" he warned as he turned on his heels and went below to get a snooze.

Jud walked aft with a broad grin on his face. He had lived dangerously ever since he was a kid in his teens and was wondering what would happen if Sir Henry knew he was the Grimsby fisherman captain that Lady Moresby had referred to in the days gone by. "Well, I guess hell would be popping right here on deck," he muttered, as Captain Henry and the Countess came up on deck. Saluting the captain and bowing to the lovely young woman, he walked back to the break of the poop as the mate had suggested whenever they came to promenade the deck.

Captain Henry remarked, smiling, as he stuck his monocle in place, "Mr. Barkley, the mate, has evidently given that lubber his orders, Catherine darling, to keep his distance when we are on deck here aft. What do you think of my new second mate? Do you think he will be going hunting in the jungles of Assaba, my dear? He asked, laughing.

"No, Henry. I do not!" she said.

After a week spent at Gravesend, the night of their departure, Lady Moresby and the Countess Catherine Du Bois came aboard the schooner. The former to wish her dear, dear friend Sir Henry bon voyage. She had left home that afternoon, telling her daughter she was going to wish Sir Henry goodbye and asked the girl if she would not care to go along with her. Her daughter said that she would not and that as her engagement at the Opera House had ended, she was going to pack up on the morrow and return to Grimsby. Lady Moresby had kissed her, stating that she would accompany her to assist her in winding up their business in that smelly town of Grimsby.

Edith would have preferred to go alone, but she nodded, then said, "Very well, mother dear."

She could not understand Jud's silence. She had not written again. Her pride prevented her from doing so. But the day before, Jack Barstow had written her, informing her that he had purchased the old Thornton home. He never mentioned one word about Judson Beasley, for since the latter had not returned to Grimsby and he had read in the papers that Edith was going to marry Sir Henry at the Villa Rosa in Naples, there was no necessity for him to do so, telling her he had left Grimsby long ago. He and Victor were angry with the Belle of

Grimsby and they had waited, day after day, to hear from their old friend Judson Beasley.

When Lady Moresby and the countess went ashore after dining with Sir Henry, and while Judson Beasley was ashore purchasing a new outfit, the former stopped at her friend's Lady Barry's and the countess drove away in Lake Moresby's victoria with a smile on her face. She stopped at Oak Lodge to see Edith and after a few moments conversation, the girl, pale of face, left the mansion on Berkley Square and returned with her to the schooner "Angel Girl." She recognized the mate immediately and was about to speak to him when boarding the schooner, when, unobserved by the countess he placed a finger on his lips and shook his head. The silent suggestion held her speechless as she went aft to the cabinet with the countess. A brooding melancholy gleamed in the blue eyes of Jim Barkley. He had taken off his cap and run his fingers through his steel-grey hair when he saw the Belle of Grimsby and wondered why the girl had come aboard the schooner on that night with the countess.

As luck would have it, he was sent ashore with Captain Henry's mail and was told by Sir Henry to hunt up the second mate as he was leaving for the Gulf of Guinea on the turn of the tide. He thought that strange inasmuch that Jud had told him she would be leaving with him to become his wife at the Villa Rosa when her engagement had ended at the theatre.

As Jim landed ashore, he caught sight of Jud who was just about hiring a boat to take him out to the schooner. Quickly he told him what had happened and what he suspected. He said that he believed Edith had been drugged for ten minutes after her arrival aboard, he had seen the girl taken to a stateroom next to that of the countess and put to bed.

Jim Barkley could never forget Jud's eyes at that moment.

"I must write to my friend Victor and Black Jack Barstow before going aboard, Jim," Jud said. "I have an idea that Edith changed her mind about marrying that blighter and in some way or other was prevailed upon to board the schooner. If Edith should recognize me when I get aboard, Jim.....Well, it's up to you to get a message to her and inform her not to do so and tell her I am known only aboard the Angel Girl as Judson Bennet, second mate."

"I can do that, Jud. But I do not believe she will awaken until we are well out at sea. I am damn sure that the girl was drugged; but why?"

"God blast him!" Beasley raged as he went to a nearby pub and penned a letter to Black Jack Barstow.

After dispatching the letter, they returned to the boat landing and shortly after were taken out to the schooner by the two Dahomey boatmen who had charge of the two bloodhounds aboard ship. As they boarded the schooner, Jud told the mate grimly, "This is going to be a hell of a trip for us, Jim, if I do not miss my guess."

Barkley wondered. They went aft just as Captain Henry came up on deck. "All aboard, Mr. Barkley," he said.

"Yes, sir!"

"Get under weigh immediately," he commanded, as he went below.

"Aye, aye, sir!" replied the mate.

When the schooner was heading down the channel, the two friends stood on the break of the poop gazing for'ard through their binoculars, while Captain Henry paced the deck aft. Barkley whispered after glancing down on the quarter deck, "we should have notified the authorities ashore before we came aboard that we believed the daughter of Lady Moresby was being abducted by Captain Henry aboard the "Angel Girl.""

Jud laughed at his assertion.

"The first thing the authorities would have done, Jim, would be to get in touch with Lady Moresby. She would have stated that Edith and the Countess went aboard the schooner to take a trip to Naples with Sir Henry, where she was going to be married shortly after their arrival there at the Villa Rosa. And, having read those facts in the papers, do you know what would have happened to us? Why, common sense should tell you, Jim, that those who accused Sir Henry Mortimer Draker of abducting the girl would land in the hoosegow—gaol. Get me?"

Barkley nodded. Captain Henry called out, "Mr. Barkley, our first port of call will be Funchal," he said. "Set the watches."

"Aye, aye, sir!" replaced the mate as Captain Henry went below to the stateroom of the countess.

"I get that!" grinned Judson. "Are you quite sure that the Belle of Grimsby is still aboard the schooner, Jim?"

"Damned sure, Jud. Dead to the world. When she opens her eyes on the morrow, she...."

"I get you! She will then discover she has been tricked by her mother or the countess into taking this trip with Sir Henry, for I am sure the darling must have changed her mind about marrying Sir Henry at the last moment."

Barkley had the graveyard watch from midnight until 4:00 am. He went below to get a smoke and think over things in general before eight bells rang out calling him on deck. He couldn't figure how in hell Jud could do anything for Edith. Jim had not a thinking apparatus in his cranium. He was first officer of the schooner and a damn good navigator; but from that night on, he took orders from Judson Beasley, the second mate—a Yankee at that. Jim would swear they never produced a better man nor yet a more likeable chap in the States and that if Sir Henry was the son of that bloody, piratical slaver he had read about, Captain Mort of the Spitfire, then the son was one of the worst scoundrels that England ever produced.

He came to the conclusion on that night that the countess, instead of being his wife, was nothing more nor less than his mistress of the sea.

At eight bells, he went up on deck to relieve Jud. He whispered before going below, "Watch your step, Jim, and don't forget a message to Edith. You can slip it through her port window, which will surely be open in the early dawn."

"I won't. But watch your step," Barkley warned.

Jud did not. The second night out he put his foot into it.

14
CONDEMNED TO DIE IN THE JUNGLES

"You God-damned Yankee bean-eater!.....When I get you ashore at the Bight of the Niger on the slave coast, I'll have my two pets, Belial and Lucifer, give you a run in the jungles there," blazed Captain Henry as he threw Jud out of the stateroom of the Countess Catherine Du Bois.

Jud permitted him to get away with it, too, for obvious reasons. He picked himself up and glared at the raging, black devil who had dropped that damned monocle from his black eye.

During his watch below, just before he was about to turn into his bunk, a soft rap came on his door and upon opening it, saw the maid of the countess standing there with a finger on her lips. She handed him a note then vanished immediately. He knew that Captain Henry was up on deck and took a chance, thinking he might learn something from her about why Edith had been brought aboard by her.

He stood frowning a moment, then asked, "What do you mean, Captain? I don't get you!"

"Get this, blast you! My two bloodhounds will be the hunters, you the hunted. Man hunting is great sport."

"It is that. Damned exciting, I should say."

Jud grinned at him then turned on his heel and ran up the companionway steps to the deck above, followed by a shot that barely missed the heel of his shoe.

After glancing at the binnacle and sails, he blazed at the man at the wheel, "Keep her full, you lubber! I'm in a hurry to get to the slave coast. I'm going hunting there. Get me?"

"Last second mate and the one before him. They no come back. Maybe more wind come and we get there quick," he said, grinning, showing his yellow fangs.

"When you go below, you damn dago, go on your knees, count your beads and pray hard for a breeze. If we don't get it, I shall know that you are the damn Jonah aboard this packet."

"What you do to me?" the man asked, insolently.

"Nothing, you damned lubber. What would I want to be doing to you—or the cutthroats for'ard?" Jud asked.

"Nothing!" the man answered, still grinning.

"Right, first guess," laughed Jud, as he walked away whistling Yankee Doodle.

Captain Henry had replaced his monocle and entered the stateroom of the countess and slammed the polished mahogany door shut. A moment later he began to berate the titian-haired, brown-eyed beauty, asking what she meant by having his second mate in her room. She was sobbing bitterly. The tears of a woman only angered him. He blazed at her, "Are you in love with that blasted Yankee? If so, 'pon my soul, Catherine, if I ever….."

She interrupted him, then laughed, and said she understood him completely.

"You meant to say, Henry, that the second mate would disappear forever in exactly the same manner as those other two mates who had incurred your displeasure. I have an idea of what became of them."

"'pon my soul, Catherine, you are a very intelligent woman. What happened to them lubbers is of no consequence. However, I assure you that both men are alive today and that they are wishing they had not butted into my affairs. But let us forget this foolishness and…"

"I will not. Leave me alone," she pleaded, as he tried to take her into his arms.

"I have a method, my dear, that never fails to work. A rebellious woman I abhor. A loving, gentle woman I worship. For two long years you have been so."

She began to sob again. "Shut up!" he blazed at her.

"I realize, Henry, that you have lied to me. You and Lady Moresby told me that you wanted to take Edith on a trip so that she might forget Grimsby and the fisherman she had fallen in love with. I realize that the blond beauty had usurped my place in your affections. You promised to set me ashore at Le Havre with twenty thousand pounds and set me free forever, if I assisted Lady Moresby in tricking her daughter to come aboard this schooner. My plan worked. Why have you broken your promise to me, Henry?" she asked, purring like a cat as she placed her arms around his neck.

"I decided otherwise at the last moment; that the daughter of my dear friend, Lady Moresby needed a chaperone. When I headed the Angel Girl for Le Havre, Catherine, I told myself that it would desolate me to part from you until Edith became my wife. Do your part in persuading her to be so and I assure you that I shall keep my promises to you—to hand over to you twenty thousand pounds and a deed to my beautiful chateau in France."

"If I fail to influence Edith, then what?"

"She shall become my mistress. You, my dear, I shall pension off," he laughed. "You shall live in luxury ever after—in the castle on the hill at Assaba." He tore her arms away from him and replaced the monocle with an air of arrogant finality.

"You black devil of hell!" she raged.

He turned and muttered with an evil smile on his face, "My dear Catherine will never see Paris again."

The shot sent after Jud had startled the mate. Silence reigned below. Sir Henry had entered his stateroom and closed the door. It was near seven bells. Jud was leaning on the cabin house gazing for'ard with a grin on his face as he watched the two blacks exercising the bloodhounds and, as always on such occasions, the men on watch were up in the rigging. The bloodhounds had been taught by their caretakers to hate them at the command of Sir Henry; therefore, no man of them had ever had the courage to desert the ship when ashore in such ports as Assaba, since two of their mates had never returned.

Jud came for'ard to the break of the poop where the mate had gone, his eyes aglow. After glancing down at the for'ard entrance to the cabinet to see if the mulatto steward was there listening, he spouted, "I have good news for you, Jim. When we get to the Bight of the Niger on the slave coast, I'm going ashore there into the jungles with them two blacks and bloodhounds trailing behind me. Great sport that!"

Jim shuddered. He was inclined to be a nervous fellow. He was five years Jud's senior, but looked much older due to the steel-grey hair of his head and the lines of sorry marked on his face. In face, he looked to be much older than Sir Henry.

"What was that shot I heard while I stood here?"

"One that hellion below sent after me as I was coming up on deck. Lallah, the Egyptian maid of the countess brought me a note from that lovely young woman requesting me to visit her. I thought I might glean some news from her, you see, so I took a chance, knowing that Sir Henry had gone up on deck. That mulatto steward must have seen me enter her stateroom and informed that black devil below of the fact."

"He did that, Jud. He came up the companionway and whispered to Captain Henry while I stood here. I saw him go below and wondered what was up."

"The countess had told me some very interesting things and when she concluded, she suddenly threw her arms around my neck and kissed me just as Sir Henry threw open her door. He caught me by the neck and threw me out and told me I was going into the jungles at Assaba with his dogs and their caretakers. Imagine that!" he grinned.

Again Jim shuddered. "I warned you to watch your step, Jud," he said, frowning.

"Well, I didn't. So what?"

"You believed what the countess told you, Jud?"

"You have another guess coming, Jim. However, I am compelled to believe some things she related to me. One thing I am sure of is this: Captain Henry will never take that lovely woman and my Edith ashore to the castle on the hill. Get that?"

"What can you or I do to prevent him from doing so with a crew like that we have for'ard? Their white uniforms do not hide the murderous looks upon their scarred faces when I give them orders. They jump at my commands and yours, but, at a word from Captain Henry, I think they would take great pleasure in cutting your throat and mine—especially them bosuns."

"I agree with you, Jim. As to what I can do to prevent him from taking me into the jungles to be torn to pieces by his pets, Belial and Lucifer, and the girls to the castle on the hill—well, I can only tell you at this time, I can do plenty. Watch me—before we reach the Bight of the Niger," he chuckled with gleaming eyes.

Keswick, England
Keswick is located in Cumbria, England in the Lake District.

15
I HATE YOU

When Jud relieved the first mate at noon, he told him that the countess had informed him that shortly after leaving the Gulf of Guinea before Sandy the mate was knocked overboard, she had heard Captain Henry mumbling while in a drunken stupor something about having a harem in the castle at Assaba.

He asked the mate if he had ever been ashore there. He said he had not. Captain Henry had sent Sandy, once in a while, up to the castle and to the overseers houses ashore near the stockades.

"I aim to enter that castle someday," Beasley told the mate as he went below.

Jim Barkley lay awake for an hour or more. He was just about to drop off to sleep when he heard someone unlock a door. He was on the port side of the ship and stuck his head close against his open window and listened. It was the first time he had heard Captain Henry talking to Edith, who had been imprisoned therein. What he heard convinced him that Jud Beasley was right in his suppositions; that Captain Henry was nothing more nor less than the black-hearted scoundrel Jud had pictured him to be.

Edith had been sobbing when he entered her stateroom. The mate could hear distinctly every word that was uttered by them. She had asked him to return to England and set her ashore. Jim did not catch what he said to her in a whisper, but he heard her ask, "Why not?"

"Why not, darling? Because I love you better than my life. When you consent to become my wife I will do so and not before. You are going to marry the richest man in England, my dear. One who will devote his life to your happiness always."

Barkley thought that Edith was thinking it over, or of the note he had slipped to her through the open port the morning after they left Gravesend that informed her Jud was aboard the Angel Girl as second mate of the schooner. He had caught a glimpse of her lovely face and saw the smile spread over it as she read the note.

He had not the slightest doubt but what she wondered about that miracle—how Jud—the man she loved had happened to be aboard the Angel Girl under an assumed name.

It was evident to Jim that Sir Henry had become impatient at the girl's silence for he suddenly blurted, "Well, my dear, say the word. Are you ready to consent to be my wife? If so, I will head back to England, calling at Le Havre where we shall be married on board this schooner. I shall leave the countess ashore there and, once in merry England, with you beside me as my beloved wife, I swear to you that I'll never leave you."

"After we were married, I would find myself as prisoner in that haunted castle of yours at Keswick ever after," she hinted.

"Don't be foolish, Edith. Dacre Castle is not haunted[2], my dear."

"It should be," she retorted laughing. "Sir Richard Tracy told me the Drakers' were never anything but pirates; men who had even murdered their own relatives."

"Some day, Sir Richard and I are going hunting in the jungles of Assaba—if you do not consent to be my wife. I have promised, on several occasion, to take him there, but so far business has prevented. However, I assure you that Dacre Castle is not haunted, my dear. Only fools believe in ghosts. I never yet saw a dead man come back to life in any shape or form. Do you believe in God?"

"I do. Furthermore, Sir Henry, I believe HE should permit ghosts to haunt some folks for they are so vile, so wicked! If what is said of the Drakers' is true, you have nothing to be proud of. When you left the navy, like your father, you disappeared from humankind for many years, Sir Richard told me. When you returned, you were fabulously

---

[2] Reportedly among the ghosts were unrequited lovers as well as kings and earls from the battlefield. For a delightful ghost story, see:
http://hauntedplacesinengland.com/dacre-castle

rich. How did you accumulate so vast a fortune—the seven years you were gone?"

"On the shores of the Caribbean and ..."

He hesitated, then laughed aloud. He was about to add something when Edith interrupted and suggested, "And on the Middle Passage, you mean. Is it not true?"

"Don't be a little fool," he flared out. "It is your mother's wish that you become my wife. When you come to your senses, we shall return to England—not before," he told her.

She commenced sobbing again. Then she broke out, "I shall never believe what the countess told me yesterday, that my mother had aided her in tricking her daughter to come aboard this schooner. She lies when she says so. If my mother visited you to wish you bon voyage as she said, I should return with her. Will you do something for me, Sir Henry?" she asked, abruptly.

"I would send this schooner with all hands to the bottom of the ocean for your dear sake," he declared.

"That is not necessary. What I ask of you is just a simple little thing. It will not entail the loss of life, I assure you."

"What is it? Your request will be granted instantly," he said.

"Kindly refrain from entering my stateroom again and go to the devil—your master!"

"Damn it!" he blazed. "You will change your mind when we get to Assaba, my girl. I tell you that I want you and by God, I will have you! As my honored wife, if so you will, as my mistress in the castle on the hill at Assaba otherwise."

"As your dear countess has been for the past two years, so she tells me. And as Lallah, her Egyptian maid, and others were before her. Go! Relieve me of your bestial presence and never again enter my room. I hate you! I loathe you! I despise you, Sir Henry, but I don't fear you!"

Sir Henry closed the door with a bang and locked it. The mate opened his door a few inches and saw Captain Henry cross the luxuriously furnished cabin and enter his own stateroom, cursing like a mad man.

From that day on the countess and Lallah, her maid, conspired with Judson Beasley day by day. Notes passed from Lallah's hand to Jud's two or three times a day. She kept him informed of what was going on in the mind of Sir Henry. But, afraid for her own life, she yielded herself, body and soul, to the man whom Edith called, "Her Friend the Devil."

Jim Barkley had very little sleep during his watch below. He went up on deck at eight bells to relieve Jud, yawning. After the man at the wheel was relieved, he went up to where Jud was standing on the break of the poop with a grin on his face. But that grin hid his feelings at that moment.

"Why the grin?" Jud asked.

Barkley was about to reply when he glanced over the rail. He turned his thumb down, then placed a finger on his lips. Jud glanced over the rail and saw the mulatto's head leaning out of the for'ard entrance to the cabinet. Gazing up at Jud, he asked, "You, Mr. Bennet, call Selim?"

"I did that, Selim…Take that and tell that hellion below how you enjoyed your reception on the quarter deck."

The steward ran back in the cabinet howling.

"If there is anything that I detest, Jim," laughed Judson Beasley, "it is tobacco chewing. I have been practicing it for the past twenty-four hours while on deck for the sole purpose of giving that steward an eyeful. When I do a job, I do a good one. Selim got an eyeful of juice that time."

"He did that, Jud, and all down his white uniform. But watch out for Captain Henry. He will come up on deck raging."

For a few moments, Barkley told Jud what he had overheard during his watch below. Jud nodded. "I get you!" he said.

Jud could barely restrain his anger when they went aft and Captain Henry came up on deck. He was half soused. He had been drinking heavily in his stateroom after his interview with the Belle of Grimsby.

He glared at Beasley, let fall the monocle and blazed, "You amuse me, Mr. Bennet."

"I'm damn glad to hear that, sir! I trust that I may be able to do so until I go hunting in the jungles, sir. My mother always said, when I was a kid, I was a most amusing boy."

"What was her maiden name, may I ask, not that I care a tinkers damn," remarked Captain Henry, with an evil glint in his eyes as he replaced the monocle and paced the deck aft.

"Jud replied immediately and lied without the least qualms of conscience, "Her name was Bridget O'Neil, sir. Born in Cork, Ireland. My father, an American of English descent. My grandfather, born at Handsworth, England emigrated with his parents at an early age."

"You amuse me again, Mr. Bennet," laughed Sir Henry.

"Do tell!" replied Jud, as he went below with a abroad grin on his face.

Barkley noted the sinister expression upon Sir Henry's face. He knew, at that moment, that Captain Henry did not believe one word that Jud had uttered, but wondered why he had not raised hell with the second mate for his action a few minutes before. Had Selim reported to him? He had, but the captain contented himself with the knowledge that in the not far distant future, he would mete out to Judson Bennet the punishment reserved for him in the jungles at the fangs of his pets, Belial and Lucifer.

Cape Finisterre
Cape Finisterre is a rock-bound peninsula on the northwest coast of
Galicia, Spain. The name is derived from the Latin name *Finisterrae*,
which literally means "Land's End".

16
OFF CAPE FINISTERRE

When off Cape Finisterre, the wind freshened up a bit and the
Angel Girl raced on carrying all sail. Later, its fury fell upon her.
The schooner made dirty weather of it. With jib and flying jib and gaff-
sails tied up and the fore, main and mizzen-spanker double-reefed she
ran southwest before it plunging bow under. She was a dandy sailor in
a light breeze that had prevailed since leaving port, but in a storm she
was the wettest thing that the two mate's had ever sailed on.

The decks were flooded all that night, but through it all Captain
Henry spent the night below in the arms of his mistress, the countess,
after telling the mates to call him only if the wind shifted.

There was no question about the men for'ard being thorough going
seamen. While in port, they had been kept hard at work, cleaning paint
work and painting her; some of the men scrubbing and holystoning the
decks; others, sewing sail or rattling down. The schooner was yacht-like
and as clean as a new pin. The guns amidships were polished day by
day and likewise the six pounder on the fo'c'sle deck, all under cover of
heavy tarpaulins, day and night.

There was not a thing for the watch on deck to do other than stand
by to jibe over the sails or take a pull on the sheets occasionally.

The two dogs Belial and Lucifer, were confined in their house that
was built adjoining the after part of the galley. Barkley's hatred of them
was not so intense as Jud's for a monstrous black cat Sir Henry had
named "Satan" that followed him all around the deck, morning, noon,
and night. It's yellow gleaming eyes in the darkness of the night

stabbed out at you. Jud had made several ineffectual attempts to grab him and throw him overboard, but the black devil avoided him.

"There will come a day, you imp of the devil, when you will disappear down the throat of a shark or I miss my guess," Beasley had grouched on that occasion.

Before going below that night, Captain Henry had told his two mates that the Angel Girl could out sail anything that ever entered the Gulf of Guinea. Jud laughed at his assertion, as did the mate, Barkley. They knew they had commanded one of the fastest boats of the Barstow fleet, one third the tonnage of the "Angel Girl."

Jud remarked, "I hope so, Captain, but in a storm, this schooner is a wet bitch. Too narrow in the beam, sir. In a calm, she almost stands still. I once sailed on a schooner, sir, that could best the Angel Girl in a calm or storm."

During the early dawn, the wind died out somewhat. The schooner was rolling from port to starboard like the wet thing she was, shipping tons of water over both rails.

Captain Henry came up smiling that afternoon and told the mates to call all hands out on deck and shake out the reefs and hoist the jibs. Later, the order came to jibe over the boom-sails and with a fair wind from the southwest the schooner headed back toward the port of Funchal.

Subsequently, everything being shipshape aboard the schooner, eight bells rang out and after the helmsman and the lookout was relieved Captain Henry went below. Fifteen minutes later he came up on deck with both ladies and began to promenade the after-deck with them. Both ladies were smiling and chatting together as though they had not a thing to worry about. A glance at their faces and one would never suspect that deep down in their hearts and souls dwelt a fear of what the future held for them. In the heart of Edith, at least, there lived a spark of hope, knowing that the man she loved—the man who idolized her—was watching over her and would, in some way or other, prevent Sir Henry from carrying out his hellish plans. She had caught a reassuring glance from Jud as she came up on deck and their eyes had met for the first time since she came aboard; but the two never had any chance of conversing with each other and never could do so under the circumstances. After dinner, she went to her stateroom where she was locked in by Sir Henry or Selim, the mulatto steward. She was waited upon by Lallah, the maid of the countess, who was still bitter toward the daughter of Lady Moresby, for not complying with Sir Henry's request—consenting to marry him would bring to her the freedom from an alliance with the man she had loved in the past but now hated with the strength of despair, even while compelled to submit to his bestial embraces.

Both mates sat at the second table. The first officer was denied the pleasure of being seated at the first table as is the usual custom. Neither men were considered worthy of the honor. However, the mates were delighted with the arrangement.

The steward, cook, carpenter and sail maker ate together. The boatswains and gunners likewise. The rest of the crew in the fo'c'sle ate there or squatted out on deck in fair weather and a more murderous looking crew of cutthroats never manned so clean and fine a ship as they.

Captain Henry, who had come up on deck smoking his bull-dog pipe after dinner that evening, paused at the binnacle then cast his eyes aloft at the sails. He beckoned to Barkley, who had gone for'ard to the break of the poop, as was the mate's usual custom when the master held the deck aft. Barkley went aft wondering what was on the black devil's mind at that moment, as Jud Beasley came up on deck and with a sly wink at the mate went for'ard to watch the two giant blacks exercising the bloodhounds. Before the captain could ask the question that had formed upon his lips, the deep, bass voice of Beasley roared out, "Hey, there, you damned lubbers! What in hell do you mean by neglecting your duties? Get after that wop whose trying to sneak back into the fo'c'sle. It's his watch on deck. I'll report you to Captain Henry and see to it that you don't ever have a chance to go hunting in the jungles with me—you black imps of hell!"

The sardonic smile on Captain Henry's face expanded into an amused grin. Then it changed abruptly and he asked Barkley, "How would you like to go hunting in the jungles with the second mate?"

"Not at all, sir! I'd sure die of the sleeping sickness there," Barkley replied, his face turning white at the question.

"Or worse," Captain Henry hinted, sardonically. "The fangs of Belial and Lucifer can tear a man to pieces in a few minutes."

"I have not the slightest doubt about that, sir," the mate replied as Sir Henry dropped the monocle from his evil eye and began to twist at his waxed moustache reflectively.

"Those dogs are man hunters. If they could speak, they would tell you what happened to men who deserted my ship at Assaba."

"I have no intentions whatever to desert, sir! I love this ship; otherwise, I would have left her in Gravesend long, long ago. If I have failed in doing my duty as first officer of this ship or as second officer under the late lamented mate, Sandy McIntosh, I apologize for doing so and will resign upon our arrival back in England."

Still glaring at Barkley, he turned on his heel and without another word went below.

Three days later, the mate dropped anchor in the roadstead at the port of Funchal, a half mile south of Fort Rock.

Neither mates expected to get liberty ashore there, but they did before weighing anchor and proceeded down the coast to the Gulf of Guinea. There, Jud learned, to his great surprise, what had happened to Bloody Pedro who had boarded the lugger Mary Jane while hove to in the Gulf of Guinea more than a year before.

Funchal, Portugal

Funchal (Madeira), Portugal: The island of Madeira is located in the Atlantic Ocean. Madeira Island is known as the Pearl of the Atlantic, the Floating Garden.

17
ASHORE AT FUNCHAL

Shortly after the anchor was dropped and the gaff-sails, jibs, staysails and fore and main were tied up, and the mizzen-spanker-sail with its great spread of canvass was left standing with the boom guyed in amidships, Captain Henry ordered the mate to take the long boat that had been lashed bottom up across the main hatch since leaving Gravesend with a half dozen men and make for the Desertas Islands to get some fresh goat's meat aboard. There was very little aboard the schooner. In fact, fish had been served on the table twice daily. The smell of it nauseated Edith. She was practically on a starvation diet.

Sir Henry had watched her continuously at the table wrinkling up that dainty, sensitive nose of hers. It amused him greatly. Had not his dear friend, Lady Moresby, told him that if her daughter got enough of it she would never care to visit Grimsby again. And, as the days went by, he firmly believed that eventually the girl would consent to become his wife and that he would be heading back to England with her. Therefore, he delayed the sailing of the schooner as much as possible. There were days that he could carry all sail in a spanking breeze when he would give the mate orders to take in the gaffs, outer jibs and staysails, much to the amusement of the second mate, Beasley.

When Jim Barkley returned loaded down with goat's meat late that afternoon, he and the second mate were sent ashore for the fruit and wines that were awaiting the schooner in the warehouse ashore.

That night, after a dinner of fresh meat, vegetables, fruits and wine was served to all hands for'ard and aft with the exception of the captain's table—fish being the order of the day for the cabin's first table, the two mates went up on deck expecting orders from Captain Henry to get under weigh again at any moment. Neither were disappointed. While Barkley wondered at the delay, Jud was jubilant. He remarked, "I hope to God we shall stay here a week or more, Jim, but I sure would like to go ashore to stretch my legs on dry land again. Maybe Captain Henry thinks that if he gave me shore liberty, I would be deserting the ship, but that black devil has another guess coming. If he set me ashore and the schooner lay in the roadstead overnight, he would find me bobbing up serenely on the deck of the Angel Girl when you set sail the following morning—yelling at his cutthroats there for'ard. You can bet your bottom dollar on that. I'd swim back to her—unless, of course, I was stuck in the hoosegow and could not make it," he grinned.

He stayed on deck for an hour or so, conversing with Barkley, telling him of his expectations before the Angel Girl arrived at the Bight of the Niger. Jim Barkley was astounded.

"Do you mean to say, Jud," he whispered eagerly, "that the schooner Jenny, under command of Black Jack Barstow and Victor Jenson will be trailing us?"

"Damn sure of it, Jim! My letter to them was a command. Get that? I own the Jenny and both them lubbers take orders from me," he said, laughing.

Barkley went below thereafter and turned in. He lay in his bunk thinking for an hour before dropping off to sleep. He, like Victor Jensen, didn't get the drift of what Jud had told him that night but shortly before closing his eyes he smiled and told himself that with a man like Jud aboard ship, there was nothing to fear from the threats of Captain Henry. In some mysterious way, the second mate would prevent him from carrying them out. But how? He could not answer that question he propounded to himself at the moment, but went to sleep with a tranquil mind.

Jud held the deck with the anchor watch until midnight. He passed by Edith's open port quite frequently, hoping she was awake and would recognize him as he whistled softly Yankee Doodle. But nothing came of it. He came to the conclusion that she was asleep or did not care to risk a word with him.

"Surely," he muttered, after pacing the alley between the rail and the cabin house, "she could write me one little note and tell me that she loved and trusted me."

He went to the break of the poop and stood there gazing shoreward and out at sea through his binoculars until eight bells rang out.

Letters were passing to him from the countess day by day, informing him of Sir Henry's plans for his and Barkley's effacement at the port of Assaba and of the captain's intentions in reference to her disposal likewise upon their arrival at the port of destination. But she seldom if ever mentioned the Belle of Grimsby in her letters. Once only, she told him that if Edith did not consent to marry him, after she herself entered the harem in the castle on the hill, Lady Moresby's daughter was destined to become the mistress of Sir Henry thereafter.

Nothing of importance happened for three long days as the schooner lay there with awnings spread aft from the mizzen-boom to protect the ladies, for they were up on deck most of the day while the mates conversed together at the break of the poop. The crew for'ard killed time by gambling out on deck in the shade of the galley house. Golden sovereigns clinked musically upon the holystoned deck that was as clean as the white uniforms those cutthroats wore; men of fifteen different nationalities. Scum of the earth.

Another day dawned, warm and sunny, but, much to the satisfaction of Judson Beasley, no word came from Captain Henry to weigh anchor and set sail. He was watching the mates who stood on the break of the poop, some thirty feet from where the ladies sat under the awning fanning themselves, Edith dressed in the borrowed finery of the countess. They stood gazing landward and glimpsed the white washed houses set in the midst of tropical verdure and at the narrow streets where ox-drawn sleds climbed the steep grades at a snail's pace, as it seemed through their binoculars.

Beyond the town stretched the terraced gardens and vineyards. And far beyond, they saw the deep ravines and gulches that cut deep into the rocky formations from which rose mountain peaks whose tops were covered with a white mantle of snow.

All around the shore stately palms nodded their heads in the gentle breeze. The two mates began to grouch like the very devil. They were grouching like a couple of polar bears in captivity; then Jud laughed and told Barkley, "I hate like the devil, Jim, to spend my time loafing around the deck here like this, but there's nothing that we can do about it. However, as I said before," he whispered, glancing over the rail to the for'ard entrance of the cabin to see that Selim wasn't there listening in, "the longer the delay the better it will be for us and the two ladies—and damn bad for the rest of the crew. And that means, for that black devil aft there.

"I'm telling you, Jim, that the Angel Girl will not drop anchor at the Bight of the Niger in the next three months—if ever."

"How come? Why not? We can make port in less than half that time with a breeze like this, Jud."

"We could, Jim. But we shall not! Sir Henry holds three aces and the joker," he laughed, as he saw the men squatted out on deck playing poker, "but I have a trick up my sleeve that I'll play when the time is ripe to do so."

Barkley wondered what kind of a trick he had up his sleeve and asked him. Jud replied with a smile on his face, "A Yankee trick—that will beat Sir Henry's play any day in the week."

"How about Sunday?" Barkley asked, as he gazed aft for a moment and saw Sir Henry still watching him and Jud Beasley.

"That black devil aft don't gamble on Sunday. You know that. He spends most of his time at the piano playing hymns or trying to coax the Belle of Grimsby to sing and play for him."

Suddenly, after winking at the mate, Jud yelled loud enough for those aft to hear him, "I wonder why Captain Henry don't give us orders to weigh anchor? I want to get into the jungles as soon as possible. I hate to hang around this god-forsaken hole."

The next moment, Captain Henry came up to the two mates with a broad grin on his handsome but devilish countenance.

"I heard what you said, Bennet. Did you ever see Satan catch a rat and play with it before killing it?" he asked, pointedly.

"No sir! I'll set a trap and catch one, down in the fore-peek, if that is possible. That will help us kill time for a half hour or more."

"'Pon my soul, you are a lubber, Bennet. To use your own words, I must say that you don't get me," he snarled.

"Lubber is right, sir. I don't get you. But why the delay? I'm damned anxious to get to the jungles and kill them dogs of yours. Get that, sir?"

Sir Henry laughed out loud. The two ladies aft glanced at him, then at the mates. The countess remarked, "Something funny amusing Sir Henry. To look at them, you would think the three of them are boon companions. But I know better, Edith."

"You should do, having been his mistress for two long years or more. However, my dear countess I think you are a fit mate for that man—Sir Henry. And…."

She paused. She had heard Sir Henry tell the mates they may go ashore, but that he expected them to return at midnight. Failing to do so, Belial and Lucifer would quickly round them up.

Captain Henry walked aft, casting back at Beasley a glance that spoke volumes.

In a half hour, they were ashore, leaving the two Negro boatmen who were the caretakers of the dogs in the boat, grinning at them.

"What in hell are you black imps of hell laughing at?" Jud blazed at them as he was about to climb up the wharf.

"You no come back, Belial and Lucifer catch you. We take back to schooner only your heads," one of the blacks said while the other sat grinning showing his white teeth.

"Someday, the sharks or alligators will get you both," Beasley threw back at them.

"I meant that, Jim. Them blacks will not live to set foot ashore at Assaba, but we shall do so, and there won't be any bloodhounds trailing us, either," he said grimly.

"Where away, Jud? I was never ashore here long enough to take in the sights of the town. Any pretty girls here?"

"You bet! But watch your step, unless you want to get a knife between your ribs. I spent a lot of time up at the big casino on Los Gatos Street. That's where I'm heading for, where I'll show you a peach of a girl all decked out in diamonds and pearls and a necklace around her neck that would bring—well, I guess about twenty thousand pounds in London. No kidding," he said, but he had no idea of what the owner of such treasures would be revealing to him that night before they left to board the schooner Angel Girl again.

18
BLOODY PEDRO'S DEMISE

They walked up the narrow street, pausing occasionally to scatter a few coins to the girls and boys that followed them after they left the boat landing. The natives—the men especially—were a lazy good-natured lot of fellas whose only object in life seemed to be that of killing time. They were dressed in short knee pants, short coats and boots that made them look so ridiculous to all foreigners who landed there at Funchal.

The girls, however, most of them beautiful, their dark brown eyes smiling at the mates, were dressed in gaudily colored skirts. Upon their black tresses that reached down to their waists, they wore blue and scarlet caps set at a jaunty angle. They followed the two men, chattering like a lot of parrots in a bazaar.

Subsequently, they entered the casino and sat at one of the tables and ordered wine. It was not like the wine they exported. It was absolutely poisonous, they thought.

Later, several lovely young girls were dancing before them, flirting with the mates. Jud grinned at them. Jim's eyes were eating them up. Captain Beasley had, night after night in that same casino killed a lot of time there before coming in contact with Barkley. His sea-green eyes sparkled when he saw the young woman he had mentioned on the way up from the boat enter the hall with her husband.

They stood behind the bar conversing together, after nodding to Jud Beasley, the man who had been exceedingly generous to the dancing girls. They recognized him immediately. They sensed the fact that both men were mates of the schooner that was anchored out in the roadstead.

Juanita De Gonzalo, still conversing in whispers with her handsome young husband, kept fingering her rings and the necklace around her lovely neck, as Jud remarked, "A handsome couple that, Jim. They are the owners of this big casino. They must be immensely rich. I wondered night after night how they got that way, but did you ever see such a beauty in your life, Jim?"

"I did, but she is a blonde, Jud. She is the fairest of the fair and I am damn sure that she is head over heels in love with a friend of mine."

"A lucky fellow, Jim. Who is he?"

"Captain Judson Beasley, a bean-eater from Boston," chuckled Jim Barkley.

"Maybe!" muttered Beasley as he beckoned to the young woman.

In the lovely girl's ears were five carat diamond earrings; on her wrist a bracelet of precious stones, and her long, slim fingers glistened with gem-studded rings.

He whispered before she rounded the bar, "What a haul for some bandit, Jim."

"I'll say so," Barkley said, as she came and stood before them. Barkley breathed inwardly, "That necklace is the very counter-part of the one that the countess wore when I boarded the schooner at Gravesend more than a year ago."

Juanita, her large brown eyes sparkling, gazed from one to the other of the mates, then asked, "Si, señors. What you wish? …Nize girls, eh?"

"No thank you!" snapped Jud. "you remember me, of course?"

"Si, señor. My husband, Ahumada, wonder where you go. We no understand. You go queek. Like that!" she said, snapping her fingers together.

"I did that! This is my friend, Mr. Barkley. I told him what a swell place you had here and we both came to pay you a visit."

"Si señor. Nize place. My first husband built it. He was very reech, but he was a fat peeg," she said, laughing.

She then informed the mates that her first man, named Pedro de Garcia, was a friend of the captain of the schooner, Angel Girl.

Jud sat up in his chair and glanced at Barkley.

"Imagine that, Jim?" he chuckled.

"Go on, please!" he encouraged her, smiling.

"One night, when el capitan came ashore a year or more ago, my husband, Pedro died."

Jud turned to Barkley. "I thought that Bloody Pedro had gone down with the Mary Jane," he whispered. "See the connection?"

Barkley nodded as the young woman, now seated between the two men, went on:

She said she had married Pedro, who was old enough to be her grandfather because it had been her parents wish; he was very rich and a power in the port of Funchal, but he was a drunken pig and she hated him. She had always loved Ahumada, her present husband. One night, when the Angel Girl dropped anchor in the roadstead, el capitan had come ashore to see Pedro. After talking for an hour at the same table where the two mates sat, he had invited Pedro to go aboard the schooner with him, stating that he wanted to give his young wife a present.

She fingered her rings and the rest of the jewelry she wore, as she told them that Pedro did not want to ever go aboard the schooner again.

Later, she said, Ahumada had entered the casino and began to dance with her. Pedro was very jealous of Ahumada. Suddenly, he rose from the table where he was seated and caught her lover by the neck and threw him outside of the casino.

In five minutes, Pedro had returned and told her that Ahumada had stabbed him and that he had had him arrested. She said that Pedro was one big liar. That he had stabbed himself, just a leetle beet. Then he told her to go aboard the schooner and get her wedding presents and say he could not come because he had been stabbed that night and was not expected to live.

She went to the boat that was waiting for Pedro and shortly after boarded the schooner and told Captain Henry what had happened, stating that her husband was a big, fat pig and a liar. Captain Henry had smiled at her and kissed her and after taking from his medicine cabinet a roll of bandages and a small vial of powder, he had accompanied her ashore. Upon their arrival at the casino, he had gone into the luxuriously furnished room and examined the wound. Then he had laughed loud and long, telling Pedro he would fix him up quick.

Without washing the wound which was but a scratch compared to those he had received on the Middle Passage, Captain Henry had rubbed into it some of the powder, then bandaged it, telling Juanita that he would be sleeping like a baby.

"He did, señors. He never wake again. I get my Ahumada free and we get married." Pedro had no brothers or sisters. No relatives. All he possessed, quite a large fortune and the casino, along with the vineyards he owned, fell into the hands of his young widow.

She was smiling happily at the mates as Jud remarked, "He was known aboard ship on the Middle Passage as Bloody Pedro, Señora. He knew too much about the captain of the schooner "Angel Girl." That is why the captain came ashore with you, since Pedro refused to visit him, and rubbed that power into the wound which enabled Pedro to go to sleep like a baby and never awaken again."

"I no understand, señor," Juanita said smiling, as she glanced at her husband.

"What you don't know won't hurt you. You are the handsomest young couple I have seen in many a day. Jim and I wish you every happiness in life and may you live long to enjoy the wealth that had been garnered so hellishly."

By this time, the casino had filled up with the best class of people in Funchal. They sat gazing admiringly at the lovely young woman and the two mates, then at the face of her husband who was all smiles.

Jud rose to his feet, then emptied his pockets out upon the table. There lay five golden sovereigns. He called the dancing girls and told them that Ahumada would exchange them and divide with them all.

He and Barkley were about to leave the casino when the girls surrounded them.

"Now what?" he barked at them.

"We kees you, señors," they chorused, simultaneously.

Jud and the mate grinned at each other as they struggled through the crowd of beauties. "Not tonight, girls. Wait until we come ashore again. Got to get back aboard ship in a hurry," he told them as they departed.

Outside, as they strolled along to the boat landing, Jud told the mate, "The schooner Angel Girl was the one that was hove to in the gulf that evening, Jim. Captain Henry figured he would be retiring from business after he met with Edith in Paris and he wanted to wipe out of existence all that knew him for what he was. First the crew of the lugger "Mary Jane," then Bloody Pedro and last of all, with the exception of them cutthroats of his now aboard the Angel Girl, was Sandy McIntosh, the mate.

"He came ashore that night to see Pedro and find out if he had carried out his orders. Pedro had hauled up the boat that trailed astern of the lugger and made his getaway aboard that coasting or fishing boat that lay hove to in the gulf.

"It is my belief he wanted to get Bloody Pedro aboard the Angel Girl and on the way up to Gravesend get him sitting upon the cabin house, as Sandy did, and then what?"

"Pedro, sensing the fact that he was next on the list to disappear from human kind had stabbed himself for the purpose of getting rid of his young wife's lover and to prevent himself from going aboard the schooner. Get that, Jim?"

"I do, by God! What a bloody murderer he is. I could never have believed it, if any one but you had told me. He is one of the most generous men. Well, Jud, he is paying me ten quid a month. Figure that out!" he said, grinning.

"I can do so. That is easy. But what I was going to say was that the powder he used, rubbed into Bloody Pedro's wound, was some deadly poison. Even into a scratch, it would kill a man quickly."

"I daresay you're right about that, Jud."

Beasley said savagely before they boarded the boat that awaited them, "I'll send Sir Henry Mortimer Draker clean, plumb into hell where he belongs, Jim!"

They found the two Negroes asleep in the boat. Jud yelled at them, "Wake up, you imps of the devil, your master, and take us aboard."

In the darkness of the night, as they sat in the stern of the boat, they saw two shadowy forms in front of them and two sets of white teeth. The blacks were grinning, thinking of the fun they would be having in the jungles hunting down the two mates with the savage bloodhounds, as they had done before when some of the crew for'ard deserted the ship at Assaba.

A half hour later the mates were aboard. Barkley called the watch on deck to hoist in the long boat.

As they went aft to the cabin Captain Henry came up on deck. He had heard the boat grind alongside of the schooner.

"Not drunk?" he questioned.

"No sir! My eyes and the mate's are wide open, sir!"

19
"YOU BEAST"

The following morning, shortly after dawn, they set sail with the northeast trade winds on the port quarter. The schooner glided south as steady as a swan. The great fore and aft sails were bellied out with the warm breeze. The men for'ard, after coiling up the ropes on deck, stood watching the shore line as they conversed together. Occasionally, they turned their gaze aft to the two mates with grins on their faces.

There was not the slightest doubt that those men knew the fate reserved for Jud Beasley and possibly for the first mate Barkley. But while Jud laughed about it, day after day, the mate himself could not help worrying. So much so, as the days went by that it was not possible for him to get a wink of sleep on his watch below in the day time. Jud knew he was nervous. Well, if there was any fighting to do, he would give Jim Barkley an easy job, he told himself.

After breakfast, Captain Henry and the two ladies went up on deck for their morning walk. Subsequently, they stood gazing through his binoculars at the distant shore line while he was telling them of this port and that. Later, while promenading on deck, the mates heard them questioning Sir Henry about the castle on the hill at Assaba.

"You will both find a welcome there with slave girls to wait upon you," he said, smiling sardonically at them. "The dancing girls, mostly Egyptian and of the Fellah tribe, are exceedingly graceful. But, my dear Edith, it is not yet too late to turn back to merry England. When we enter the Gulf of Guinea, it will be. I shall not then.....Well, just say the word, Edith, and I'll bout ship and head for Le Havre."

"Please do!" pleaded the countess.

Edith ignored her. "I never expected to enjoy this trip, Sir Henry, but I assure you that I do so. And, now that I am aboard the Angel Girl—not of my own free will of course—I am more desirous of visiting that famed castle of yours on the slave coast. If turning back depends upon my consenting to become your wife, Sir Henry, then I assure you that I would much rather be at the bottom of the ocean."

"I have told you repeatedly," she declared, heatedly, "that I hate you, loathe and despise you. What more can I say?"

"I never knew a girl who did not change her mind at the last moment, Edith," he lied. "you have much to learn—yet!"

"Had you a spark of love in your heart for me, Sir Henry," Edith said bitterly, "you would have granted my request to take me ashore at Funchal to see the sights there. Is it possible that you thought I might seek the British Consul and appeal to him for protection from you?"

"No, my dear. The consul there, Bruce McDonald, is a very dear friend of mine. "My influence placed him there," he said, grinning evilly at her.

"I permitted my two mates to go ashore to give them a chance to run around with the lovely girls there—girls who are ever ready to throw themselves into the arms of any white man for a few shillings. I have not the slightest doubt about it that both mates had a jolly good time with one or the other girls they found dancing in the casinos."

"You beast!" Edith flared. "Your suggestions are vile. Your heart as black as the devil—your master, and...."

"Why," he interrupted her, "what would you have? Sailors are sailors, my dear. In every port of call they have a girl."

Jud glared unseeingly at the mate with fists clenched. He got up from the table scowling. He glared up the companion way as he muttered, "His insinuations are almost unbearable, Jim. I have half a mind to....."

"Easy goes it, Jud." Barkley warned. Don't make any such foolish move. Calm down, mate what in the devil could I do alone for the girls if you were in irons below deck?"

"Righto, Jim. I've got to listen to such palaver and take it for their sake. But...."

"But what, Jud?"

Beasley evaded the direct question. He glared at the mate out of those mysterious eyes of his a moment than glanced around the cabin as though in search of some weapon or other, then ran up on deck.

He cast a hurried glance at the two ladies who avoided him, then up at the sails. He went for'ard to the break of the poop and stood glaring at the men on deck for a few moments when Captain Henry barked at him, "Trim the head sheets and take a pull on the foresail halyards, Mr. Bennet."

"Aye, aye, sir!" replied Jud, as he dropped to the main deck and bawled out the order to the bosun on watch.

It was Barkley's watch below. He went to his room and turned in to his bunk. There he lay for nearly three hours, thinking thoughts that were bitter indeed.

He heard the girls come below and enter their staterooms. Captain Henry remained up on deck for a half hour longer to finish his smoke. He heard stealthy footsteps passing his door. He peeked out and saw the mulatto steward turn a key in the lock of Edith's door then replace the key in his pocket. He wanted to go out and choke the life out of him. He padded away, for'ard to the galley to give the cook his orders. Lallah, the Egyptian maid, left her room and entered that of the countess, where the latter was then occupied with writing a letter.

When off Cape Verde, as he could not sleep on that day as he lay with closed eyes, he suddenly rose from his berth, dressed and went up on deck at seven bells. There he found Jud, as usual, on the break of the poop gazing out of his binoculars at the coast line and then out at sea. As Barkley stood by his side, after a glance aft, he whispered, 'See anything of the "Jenny?"

"No, Jim. But I'm not worrying," he chuckled, glancing over the rail, forgetful of the fact that the mulatto steward was for'ard in the galley. "She is bounding along at a fourteen knot clip in this breeze, Jim. If she don't heave in sight before we reach the gulf—well, you don't need to worry about that. I have told you repeatedly, I believe, that I have a trick up my sleeve, and, by God, when in the gulf-near land, I'll play it!"

"I'm wondering all the time what kind of a trick you have concealed."

"I told you before, Jim, that it was a Yankee trick that will beat that devil aft and prevent him landing us and the girls ashore. What more could you wish for?"

"Nothing!" the mate said. "But what are you going to do?"

"I'm going to make things in general aboard this schooner pretty damned hot for him and them lubbers for'ard. You can bet your boots on that," he chuckled, as the Captain went below.

Jud and Barkley went aft to the wheel. The former whistling Yankee Doodle, unconcernedly.

They saw the steward run aft to set the table and as eight bells rang out, Sir Henry and the ladies became seated in the cabin. Fish chowder—fish soup, the steward called it—was served first. Then fried fish and fish salad. Edith sat wrinkling up her nose as usual which brought a smile to Sir Henry's face always. He loved fish and so did the countess, but even she had become tired of it and ate sparingly. The daughter of Lady Moresby contented herself with eating the rolls and marmalade that was always placed on the table. Her face was pale, but as beautiful as ever. She had lost ten pounds in weight on the trip. She was just about half starved and almost, but not quite, ready to devour the fried fish that nauseated her at all times. Her stubborn disposition had prevailed and prevented her from doing so.

While Captain Henry was up on deck and the mates sat at the second table, the steward went for'ard for some goat's meat which he served as an addition to a large platter of fried fish and vegetables. Lallah came out of the room of the countess with a furtive glance around the cabin as she glided over to Judson Beasley and handed him a note—the letter that the countess had been writing while Barkley was in his bunk during his watch below.

After dinner, Jud went to his room while the mate went up on deck. He closed and locked his door, got into his bunk, after closing his port window to prevent Sir Henry from peering in upon him, and then read the letter. He grinned and frowned repeatedly while doing so, as he read:

"My brave and noble friend. While you were ashore with the mate having a jolly good time with the girls ashore, Sir Henry told me that you and Mr. Barkley were both going into the jungles when we drop anchor at the Bight of the Niger. Other men have, during the two years I have sailed aboard this schooner and they never returned. What became of them I do not know. Sir Henry said they had deserted the ship and they had made their way across those steaming jungles infested with alligators in the swamps and probably arrived at some French port. I do not believe him. He sent those two Dahomey blacks after them with the bloodhounds and they came back the following day laughing and reported to Sir Henry. I heard him say on that occasion that it would be a lesson to the rest of the crew for'ard. What became of the last two second mates, previous to Mr. Barkley coming aboard, God only knows.

"Edith refuses to marry Sir Henry. She says she will die first. Death would be preferable to us both, rather than life in his harem at the castle on the hill—if there is such. He is such an abominable liar that I do not believe him, even while it is quite possible that he may be telling the truth; for I know that he has transported girls there since I have been his mistress aboard here. I beg of you to save me from a fate that is worse than death. To give Lallah some weapon or other for me, that I may be able to defend myself from the man who betrayed me shortly after we left Le Havre two years ago. I am sick unto death and implore you to do something to prevent him from carrying out his threats.

"Can't you and Mr. Barkley do something—stir up the crew for'ard and take charge of the schooner and head back to Le Havre before it is too late. There, I swear to you, Jud, that I will dispose of my chateau and other property that I own and leave with you for America, as your wife or mistress. No matter which, I assure you, as God is my judge, I will be yours through eternity.

"Lovingly yours, Catherine"

After reading that letter which nauseated him, bringing a deep frown upon his face, he told himself that she had not one thought for the safety and happiness of the daughter of Lady Moresby.

He muttered, "Why in hell, if she wanted to escape from his bestial embraces, she did not leave him at Le Havre with Sir Richard Tracy and his bride, or even before. She certainly had lots of chances to do so in the past two years. I dare venture to assume that she had assisted him in tricking other beautiful girls to come aboard the Angel Girl as she had in tricking Edith. Well, she is playing a game and so am I and I'll see to it that neither one or the other of these girls aboard here ever enter that castle," he declared, grimly.

When he went up on deck at eight bells that afternoon, Captain Henry was below deck with the countess. He and Jim walked to the break of the poop out of hearing of the man at the wheel. There he told Barkley of what the countess had said in her letter to him.

"You believed her?" Barkley asked.

"I did and then again, I didn't, Jim. The letter contains some truth; but she never gave a thought to my darling's future. She was not concerned a bit as to her welfare. But it is quite obvious to me that we must prevent them from landing in the castle on the hill. That is not only a possibility but a practical certainty, whether the Jenny overtakes us or not. You may gamble on that, Jim, and you will win," he said, vehemently.

Several weeks after leaving Funchal, as the schooner headed into the Gulf of Guinea, Captain Henry came up on deck and barked at the two mates, "Haul down the jib and flying jib. Clew up the gaffs and staysails."

"Aye, aye, sir! Expect a tropical storm, sir?" asked Jud, respectfully.

"No, you damned lubber! I'm in no hurry to get to Assaba. Are you?" he asked, pointedly.

"Yes sir. Absolutely! I want to stretch my legs out there in the jungle."

He grinned at the mate as he went for'ard to carry out Captain Henry's orders. When all was snug and shipshape again, he returned to the break of the poop. He stood a moment glancing around the gulf, then turned on his heel as Sir Henry called out for both mates. They went aft and faced him.

"It is quite possible, gentlemen, that I shall be heading back to Gravesend in a week or ten days. But neither one of you two men will be aboard this schooner. After we drop anchor at the Bight of the Niger, you may have liberty ashore there and go hunting every day in the week."

"Why not on Sunday, sir?" asked Jud, smiling.

"Why not, you damned lubber! Because that is the Sabbath—a day of prayer," he said, with an evil grin upon his face.

"Yes sir! Quite true, sir! I get you sir! And, I am quite sure that Mr. Barkley understood you, too, sir!"

Barkley remained silent. His face was pale, but in the depths of his heart he was chuckling inwardly at Jud Beasley's respectful, but ready answers.

Captain Henry, dropping his monocle from his eye, glared at both mates for a moment then went below. Before the two mates had time to utter a word to each other, the deep, bass voice of the devil rang out in song as he pounded the ivories, singing some of his favorite hymns.

"It won't be long now," whispered Beasley to the mate.

"Long for what, Jud?"

"Before that damned hypocrite fetches up in hell!"

Dacre Castle

Dacre Castle is a quadrangular building with four turrets, a pele tower design that was built around the time of Henry VII. The castle was restored as a private dwelling in 1688 and by 1816 was being used as a farmhouse. [3]

As a pele tower rather than a castle, it has walls seven feet thick and 66 feet high, and has 3 notable floors. There are numerous haunted ghost stories about the castle. [4]

---

[3] http://www.lakedistrictwalks.net/dacre-castle-pooley-bridge

[4] http://hauntedplacesinengland.com/dacre-castle

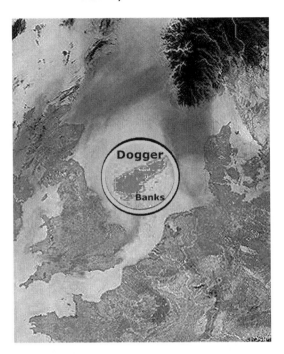

Dogger Banks is a large sandbank in a shallow area of the North Sea about 62 miles off the east coast of England. It extends over approximately 6,800 square miles, with its dimensions being about 160 miles long and up to 60 miles broad. The water depth ranges from 49 to 118 feet, about 66 feet shallower than the surrounding sea. It is a productive fishing bank. The name comes from dogger, an old Dutch word for fishing boat, especially for catching cod.[5]

---

[5] http://en.wikipedia.org/wiki/Dogger_Bank

20
THE SEA RANGER

That evening, a breeze from the southwest sent the Angel Girl toward her destination. She glided along like a swan with the wind on her starboard quarter—heading directly for the Bight of the Niger. Captain Henry had felt the schooner listing over to port and went up on deck immediately.

The mates knew quite well why he had delayed the schooner's arrival, so far; but Barkley did not understand his actions on this day. They were absolutely confusing to him but not to Judson Beasley, inasmuch as the countess still kept him informed of Sir Henry's future actions. Jud was even then reading a note from her that Lallah had handed to him. He was grinning like the devil as he heard Captain Henry tell the mate to set the topsails, jibs and staysails; shake out the reefs of fore, main, and mizzen.

Jud got up from his bunk, shaved, washed, and dressed. At one bell, he stood before his mirror grinning. At eight bells, he turned on his heels, glanced around, then ran up on deck. He glanced at the big sails bellied out with the wind that was refreshing indeed, for down in the cabin in his room, he had been roasting with the sun shining on his side of the ship during his watch below.

"This is great!" he muttered, loud enough for Captain Henry to hear him. "Soon, very soon, I'll be ashore there at Assaba."

He started to go for'ard when Captain Henry bawled at him, "Don't be so sure of that, Mr. Bennet. Remember what I said about catching a rat and playing with him?"

Eight bells rang out fore and aft as Jud replied, "I do, sir!"

"Go for'ard and take in the jibs, topsails and staysails and double reef, fore, main, and mizzen."

"Yes, sir. Aye, aye, sir!" replied Jud, a smile on his face. His mutterings had accomplished the desired effect. He was jubilant, but not so the men for'ard. One of them bleated, "Hell, we get enough exercise running up the rigging out of reach of them damn dogs."

"You'll be getting more before you fellows ever reach the Bight of the Niger, mark my word for that. No loafing on the job. Get hold of that downhaul, you scum. If I were captain of this schooner, I would string you up by the thumbs and have one of them blacks give you a score of lashes on the bare back with them whips they carry around with them."

"Like hell you would!" the man said, insolently. "What in hell do you think my mates would be doing, Mr. Bennet—looking on while you were laughing and enjoying the fun?"

"Just that, my man. No man would dare raise a hand in your behalf. Get me?"

The man scowled at him. "Sure! When things are shipshape. I've had a notion to wipe up the deck with you before you go ashore. I asked Captain Henry's permission to do so last night when I was at the wheel. Just wait until....."

Barkley came for'ard having heard the man and told him to get busy or he would clap him in irons. The man scowled at him and went to work, sending murderous glances back at the second mate, as the countess and Edith came up on deck.

"Jim," he whispered, "this little by-play was staged by that black devil aft for the benefit and edification of the ladies. That insolent devil, I was informed by the countess, is an old time bruiser of the navy. He just told me that Captain Henry gave him permission to wipe up the deck with me."

"By God, Jud! I'd hate to see you get mauled up by him. He is the bully of the fo'c'sle, you know."

"I'll knock it out of him," Jud told him, laughing.

The men worked like troupers, jumping around like so many monkeys, while Jud yelled out his orders at them. Captain Henry and the ladies were watching their actions. He commented, "There's a man that can handle men, ladies. I dare venture to assume that he has sailed on many a hell ship and that he never handled the crews for'ard with kid gloves."

He chuckled, then went on, "My men for'ard are as gentle as so many ewe lambs."

Edith told him, "They look like a lot of murderers, Sir Henry, and I wouldn't be a bit surprised to learn that each and every one of them were—well," she smiled, "those uniforms they wear that you furnish them with, like those of sailors on yachts I saw, does not hide from me their...."

She was watching the men while speaking. The job was done and the mate and Barkley were walking aft together when the bully of the fo'c'sle caught hold of Jud's arm, turned him around and sent in a blow to the jaw. Had it landed, Jud would have landed in the scuppers and remained there. But he ducked, sent in a left hook and then a right to the man's jaw that bowled him over on his back. But he did not stay there. Astonished, he rose to his feet with the blood streaming from his mouth and rushed in like a bull, head first, with his brawny arms ready to grasp Jud and crush him. Again, Jud sidestepped and sent in two crushing blows that sent the man to the deck with a groan of agony upon his lips. He stayed there, bleeding from nose and mouth. Jud bawled at him, "Get up, you scum of the Middle Passage!" to the men who had stood around them, grinning, he yelled, "Wash down decks!"

Each and every man jumped at the command. Jud and Barkley walked aft and shortly stood on the break of the poop watching the lubbers as they hustled around the deck with brooms and pails, drawing water from over the side of the schooner. The first few buckets, however, were thrown at the bully of the fo'c'sle, followed by roars of laughter from his mates.

"I told you ladies," chuckled Captain Henry, "that Bennet was a man who could handle men." The countess smiled. Edith frowned at him, then told him, "I have not the slightest doubt about it, Sir Henry, that Mr. Bennet could handle you likewise—in a fair fight."

Sir Henry frowned at her. "If I were not captain of this ship, I..."

"You would not dare to tackle Mr. Bennet," she said, as she went below with the countess, leaving him standing by the helmsman, glaring for'ard at Judson Beasley.

He had hoped to see his second mate come aft, crawling on hands and feet upon the poop deck. He was more astonished at the outcome of that fight than even his crew for'ard. Barkley, knowing that Jud had licked the bully of the fleet back in Grimsby, had been fearful that the men for'ard would have manhandled Beasley and had come prepared to aid him; for in his belt he carried a gun, concealed from Sir Henry's gaze, however.

Captain Henry went below. They heard a door slam, then a curse from Sir Henry, followed by the laughter of the Countess Du Bois.

"What a disappointment that must have been to you, Henry," she sneered, "Mr. Bennet certainly gave you a great surprise. Be honest now. Admit that you were so."

"I do, Catherine. He is a man!"

"And yet you would dispense with his services by sending him into the jungles to his death. How foolish of you, Henry. You will need a navigator on the return trip. Have you a man for'ard who could take the places of your mates, aft?"

"I have. Two men. Those bosuns are both navigators," he lied.

He admired the second mate, but at the same time, he feared him. He had asked himself repeatedly, "Where in hell have I seen that man Bennet before or some man he resembles?"

"Jim," Jud was saying, "hell will be let loose aboard here when we are a little north of south of Annobón Island. Get me?"

Barkley nodded, but he wondered as he had all down the coast, what kind of a hell Jud meant.

The night passed quietly and the following day likewise. The wind had almost died out. In the gulf they sighted a few small coasters hugging the land. Out at sea, far to the west, a trailing cloud of smoke. Barkley told Jud that perhaps his letter to Black Jack Barstow had miscarried.

"If so, Jim, it's up to us to do the best we can and prevent the Angel Girl from reaching Assaba, as I have told you repeatedly. She will never drop anchor at the Bight," he muttered, grimly, as Captain Henry came up at deck smoking.

"Mr. Barkley," he called, "if this little breeze holds out we shall drop anchor at the Bight next Sunday. But, as that is the Sabbath, we shall not land ashore there until the following morning, after eating a hearty breakfast.

"On Sunday night, as is my usual custom you know, we shall give thanks to God in the cabin below, for having brought us safely, once again, to the land where you and Mr. Bennet may have liberty ashore there."

"That is stale news, Captain. Tell us two lubbers what is on your mind," Jud bantered.

"Call all hands aft, Mr. Barkley," he commanded, as he came to the break of the poop and stood scowling for'ard as the mate passed the order along to the bosun.

Less than three minutes later, all hands stood on the quarter deck gazing up into the faces of the three men. Jud was grinning at them. Some of the men, thinking of the licking he had given the bully of the starboard watch, grinned back at him.

"My bully boys," said Captain Henry, gazing into the faces of his men, "this is my last trip to the gulf. My two mates wish to go hunting in the jungle. All you men will remain aboard ship. We shall remain at the Bight about three days. From there, we are bound to Naples, Italy. I shall pay you off in that city, adding one thousand dollars bonus for faithful service. The Angel Girl will be sold at that port and each and every man of you will then go your way in peace and sin no more," he concluded, smiling.

Every damn lubber of them cutthroats laughed uproariously at his quip.

Sir Henry held up his hand for silence. The din subsided immediately, as he spouted again, "That is all I have to say, my bully boys. Grog ho!"

They roared again. The ladies down below wondered what was going on—on deck. Edith was locked in her stateroom, but the countess came up on deck and saw Sir Henry and the two mates together. She could not imagine what was going on for she could not see that the crew was mustered aft. She went below again, fuming.

When the racket on the quarter deck subsided, Captain Henry remarked, "There is not the least chance, Mr. Bennet, for you or the mate to stir up a mutiny aboard my ship. I know my men. One word from me and they would tear you two lubbers to pieces."

"I'll tell the world that you know your men," admitted Jud, ruefully. "Anyway, I assure you, sir, that Mr. Barkley and I don't aim to do a damn thing to spoil your fun; but I assure you also that I can hypnotize those damn dogs of yours and after they have settled with them two black care-takers, make them return aboard the schooner and jump at your throat. That would be great sport."

Barkley held his peace, while Captain Henry spouted, "A few years ago, Mr. Bennet, nothing would have given me more pleasure than to have had a man of your caliber by my side; but things have changed. I could have wished a better fate for you than what awaits you both," he chuckled.

"I don't, Captain. I'd rather take my chances ashore in the jungle then remain aboard this ship with the noble Sir Henry Mortimer Draker, whose hands are dyed red with the blood of a hundred men."

The evil glitter in the eyes of Captain Henry unnerved the mate. He likened them to a deadly rattler's who was about to bury his fangs into that which had disturbed him. He was certainly disturbed at that moment by Jud's remarks. But he replaced the monocle he had let fall a moment before and smiled evilly as he turned away.

"I hit him in a tender spot, Jim. He did not know that I knew him to be other than Captain Henry, you see."

"I know. I saw the startled look upon his face," the mate said as he went below to turn in.

Four hours later, when Barkley went up on deck to relieve Jud, he found him by the rail astern. Jake Bradley, the man the second mate had given a beating to was at the wheel listening in. Jud knew he would report to Captain Henry every word they said and probably add a lot they did not. He lowered his binoculars and beckoned Barkley for'ard. There, at the break of the poop, he whispered after glancing over the rail, "Look at that two-masted schooner astern there, Jim. What do you make of her?"

The men for'ard were up in the rigging watching her as Barkley gazed long and earnestly at the schooner, then lowered his glasses.

"She is the Sea Ranger," he sighed, regretfully.

"I think she is just what she ain't," laughed Judson Beasley, as eight bells rang out fore and aft.

Sons of the Sea
"Sons of the Sea" is a traditional sea shanty with many versions and varied lyrics.

21
WHAT SHIP IS THAT

The mate turned away disappointedly.

"I tell you, Jim, that schooner is just what she ain't. Get me?"

"No. you said that before. I don't get the drift of it," grouched the mate, as he gazed into the gleaming eyes of Beasley.

"Listen, you lubber! I'll bet you a hundred dollars—twenty quid—that she is the "Jenny." That she is commanded by either Victor Jenson or Black Jack Barstow."

Barkley grinned at his assertion. "By God, I think you would win, Jud. The name on her bow confused me, somewhat, even while I wondered if it was possible that..."

Before Barkley could finish, there rolled out over the gulf the deep, bass voices of the men aboard the schooner. The mates went aft and trained their binoculars on her again. The crew of the "Sea Ranger" broke out into song. They were singing an old song Jud had heard every time he had headed into the port of Grimsby, loaded down with fish. Down in the cabin below, Edith suddenly sat up and with smiling face, listening ears at her port window she heard, as she had in the past, the song that thrilled her and the two mates on deck. The men on the "Sea Ranger" were singing:

"Have you heard the talk of foreign powers,
Building ships, increasingly?
Do you know they watch this Isle of ours —

They watch this Isle unceasingly?
But there's one thing they forget — they forget!
Our boys in blue they have met — they have met!

SONS OF THE SEA, all British born,
Sail on every ocean, laughing foes to scorn.
They may build their ships, my lads,
　And think they know the game;
But they can't beat the boys of the bull-dog breed,
　That have made old England's Name!

Have you heard of the things that they now do —
　Strengthening their fleets and why?
Our British ships are all built of oak,
　In battle we dare do, or die.
But there's one thing they forget — they forget!
Our boys in blue they have met — they have met!

SONS OF THE SEA, all British born,
Sail on every ocean — laughing foes to scorn.
They may build their ships, my lads,
　And think they know the game;
But they can't beat the boys of the bull-dog breed,
　That have made old England's Name!

Smiling, the two mates turned to gaze for'ard. There stood Captain Henry at the entrance to the cabin with his glasses trained on the schooner.

"One of her majesty's sloops out looking for coasting slavers. When they see one, they run away from her," he laughed.

"If she happens to be owned by some British Lord or Duke, or even a baronet," Jud said, with a broad grin on his face.

The shot went home. Captain Henry let fall the monocle from his eye, glared at Jud a moment, then replaced it and laughed outright.

"That is quite possible, Mr. Bennet. For a Yankee, you seem to know quite a lot—too much, in fact, to please me," he said significantly.

"I agree with you, sir. But I assure you, sir," declared Beasley, respectfully, "that ashore in the jungle I shall forget everything, especially that which…"

He broke off abruptly. Captain Henry blazed at him, "'Pon my soul, Bennet, you never uttered a truer word. You will certainly forget everything you ever knew, and…."

He was cut short by the captain of the "Sea Ranger" that was now abreast the Angel Girl about three ship's length away, yelling, "What ship is that? Hey there!….Ship ahoy! Are all you lubbers dead aboard there?"

Barkley was about to reply when Captain Henry spouted, "This is the Angel Girl from Southampton, England. A pleasure craft sailing the seven seas, bound to the Bight of the Niger to go hunting in the jungles there with my two mates. What schooner is that?" he asked, his voice grating harshly upon the ears of the captain and his mate aboard the "Sea Ranger."

Something told Jud he was suspicious of the strange schooner. A moment later a voice roared, "This is the "Sea Ranger". A smuggler. Captain Jacob Bluff in command. The customs officers at Penzance made it too damned hot for me there. I thought I might pick up a little easy money at Las Palmas, but there was a blasted British government boat anchored in the roadstead. Chased me down the coast as far as Cape Verde, but I ran out to sea and gave her the slip. I'm now heading for the gold coast to see what I can pick up there. Know anything about that country?" the voice of Black Jack Barstow yelled, as the little schooner was passing the Angel Girl at a fast clip.

"Lots of gold there. Go to it, me hearties, and good luck to you!" Captain Henry bawled back with an evil grin on his face.

"Thanks! But say, who is captain of that schooner?"

"Captain Henry. Yours?"

"I told you once. Go to hell! I'll see you in the gloaming—on the slave coast—maybe!"

"I daresay, and when I do see you, I'll ram my fist down your throat, damn you!" blazed Sir Henry.

"I'll see you in hell first," boomed the voice, faintly.

Jud whispered to the mate out of the corner of his mouth. "That was Black Jack Barstow, Jim."

"I know it, Jud. But I did not see Victor aboard her. Look at Captain Henry's face. It's a wonder he don't turn the guns on the "Jenny."

"If the countess and Edith were not aboard, they would be belching hell at her right now," Jud stated, confidently.

He was right. Absolutely correct. Captain Henry snarled, "But for my lady guests below, I would send that insolent devil of a smuggler to the bottom of the gulf. Jibe the mainsail, Mr. Barkley."

"Aye, aye, sir!" Barkley sang out as he went for'ard to the break of the poop, paused there a moment then went down to the main deck just as Captain Henry yelled at the helmsman, "Luff, damn you! Where in hell is that blasted smuggler going?

Let go your jib halyards, lower away the foresail. God blast him, he will take our jib-boom off. Hey there! Sea Ranger, ahoy! What in the devil do you mean by crossing my bow? Are you lubbers drunk aboard there?"

"Not yet!" yelled Black Jack, as he stood on the rail clinging to the rigging. "This is my birthday. Just celebrating it. But them blokes for'ard are raising hell with a stowaway that sneaked aboard of my ship before leaving port. They distracted my attention for a moment. Starboard!" he yelled at the helmsman, as Jud and Barkley, with binoculars trained on the men for'ard saw at a glance what had happened.

The next moment Black Jack had bounded from the poop to the main deck with cutlass in hand. He ran for'ard, just as a man sprang upon the rail and yelled for help, the next moment he took a header into the sea. Shots flew around him as he dived under repeatedly and swam toward the Angel Girl.

"Throw that man a line," barked Captain Henry, as the little schooner sheered off and, with the light breeze, bounded away in the direction of the gold coast.

"Run up the jibs and foresail, Mr. Barkley," yelled the captain who was furious, undoubtedly at the insults hurled at him by a common smuggler.

Jud was on the main deck standing by to throw the swimmer a line. On his face was a broad grin. The mate stood a few paces for'ard of him. While hurling his commands at the watch on deck, he glanced aft and saw Sir Henry pacing the poop-deck raging like the devil he was, glancing occasionally through his glasses at the schooner ahead.

The Angel Girl was moving at a snail's pace as Jud hauled the swimmer aboard. His face was turned for'ard and seeing Barkley, he closed one eye. The mate grinned, for he immediately recognized his old friend, Victor Jenson.

Barkley sensed the fact that something was doing. What, he could not imagine. He told himself, while chuckling inwardly, that perhaps Victor, too, had a trick up his sleeve—one that he preferred to deliver to Jud Beasley, personally. He was absolutely right in believing so, for Captain Black Jack and Victor had made several plans for boarding the Angel Girl and taking from her the daughter of Lady Moresby.

As Jud assisted Victor aft, who was, apparently, exhausted, he muttered, "Get a message to Edith. Tell her not to recognize me and not to worry."

"Belay, there! Run up the foresail and be quick about it, you blasted lubbers!" the mate yelled at the men, for he was so anxious to get aft to see what would happen next.

"'Pon my soul, man. Them smugglers hated you. Why?"

"I daresay the shoe was on the other foot, Captain," Victor told him, as he turned to gaze for'ard, apparently at the schooner far ahead, but winking at his friends who stood behind him. Turning back to face Captain Henry, he remarked, "If you were a navigator, sir, and had been shanghaied as I was, as I lay on the dock drunk as a Lord, you would not feel like loving that yelping lot of smugglers aboard that schooner, would you?" he asked, pointedly.

"I daresay not. But it seems to me that the captain of her is a damn poor marksman. One of those shots should have nipped you."

"Captain Jacob Bluff was about three sheets in the wind, sir. He was cockeyed. He could not have hit an elephant," he chuckled.

"Mr. Barkley, go for'ard and see if you can bring down his mainmast," he commanded.

"Aye, aye, sir!"

He went for'ard grinning. Had Captain Henry told one of the expert gunners to do that, it was evident to Jud and Barkley that it might have happened. Barkley trained the gun himself, while some of the crew stood by. He missed. A moment or so later, the schooner Jenny luffed. One of the six pounders barked. A flash, a puff of smoke and a shot struck the flying jib-boom and brought down the headsail. Barkley was about to send another shot when Captain Henry yelled, "Avast there!

I'll board that lubber some dark night and send them all and the "Sea Ranger" to the bottom."

Victor muttered inwardly, "You will like hell!" the next moment he blurted, "I pray to God that I may have the pleasure of boarding that schooner with you, sir."

"You may, sir, I assure you that we shall wipe out every jack man of them damned smugglers," he declared, vehemently, as he beckoned to Victor to follow him below.

When the two mates were together, Jud whispered, "All serene, Jim. The ladies licked the devil."

"Your watch on deck, Jud. I'm going below, while you and the men get busy on that wreckage, for'ard. But for the fact that I am a damn poor gunner, I might have brought down the mainmast of that gallant little schooner. I say I might, understand?"

"Sure! I get you, Jim. Listen in a bit, if possible," he whispered, as he ran for'ard and began to hustle the men around the deck, sending a half dozen of the cutthroats out on the end of the jib-boom to clear away the wreckage.

As Barkley went below to his room, he mused, "I wonder if the two tricks my friends' carry up their sleeves will outwit those of Captain Henry's? With a crew like that for'ard, what in hell can we three men do to circumvent his plans—that of landing the girls at the castle?"

Captain Henry had no intention whatever of taking the daughter of Lady Moresby to the castle on the hill. He visualized himself living in his villa at Naples with the girl herself and waiting there for the arrival of Lady Moresby in accordance with the plans they had made before she left the schooner at Gravesend. However, he was determined to get rid of the Countess Catherine Du Bois on his last trip to the gulf.

Annobon Island
Located in the Gulf of Guinea.

22
A SURLY BLIGHTER

After Jud had finished his work on the deck for'ard, he went aft and stood alongside the helmsman, gazing at the sails and binnacle, occasionally, but was in fact, listening in to the conversation that went on below decks.

Far beyond, almost out of sight swallowed up by the haze on the gulf, he could see the Jenny heading up to the slave coast with Annobon Island but five miles ahead of her.

Barkley, the mate, in his cabin below, was wondering what chance Black Jack Barstow and his men had of boarding the Angel Girl when she dropped anchor at the Bight. Surely, he told himself, very little; for a hundred blacks would be coming out from the stockades in their swiftly moving proas. Knowing that was possible, he groaned inwardly and believed that every one aboard the schooner Jenny would be wiped out of existence and the schooner he loved sent to the bottom of the gulf after he, Jud, and Victor had their throats cut from ear to ear by the vicious crew for'ard at the command of Sir Henry.

Down below, Jud heard Captain Henry saying, "Captain Simpson, my suit fits you like....well, as if it was made for you."

"It does that, sir. I certainly appreciate your kindness, but I wish you had turned all the guns loose on that blasted smuggler."

"Some dark night when that smuggler least expects us, as I said before, you shall have a chance to wipe out the insults heaped upon you. Not one man shall escape, I assure you. The Sea Ranger will find a resting place at the bottom of the gulf, where, in the past, I have sent many such who ran afoul of me. But for the ladies I have aboard ship, she would be at the bottom, long ago, with all hands."

"Ladies aboard, sir?" Victor exclaimed, apparently amazed at Captain Henry's assertion. "Is it possible? In such times as these, I would not risk the life of my wife on my coasting vessel. Furthermore, I doubt, sir, that your men for'ard would have an easy time of it tackling those fellows aboard the Sea Ranger in daylight. They are the toughest lot of blood-thirsty men I have seen in many a long day and I have run up against a lot of them in my time. I hope we shall meet them face to face again."

"We shall, sir." Captain Henry assured him, grimly, as they came up on deck. Jud Beasley went for'ard as usual to the break of the poop with a broad grin on his face.

"Who is that lubber, Captain?" asked Victor, loudly, nodding in the direction of his friend, Jud Beasley.

Sir Henry dropped the monocle from his eye. He gazed at Jud, evilly. "That is my second mate, Mr. Bennet. He and the mate, Jim Barkley, wish to go hunting in the jungle upon our arrival at the Bight. I gave them my word of honor that they should have that privilege for three days, but," he whispered, chuckling inwardly, "I firmly believe that both men will be deserting my ship and, therefore, never return to her again. I have been worried greatly about that, but since your arrival aboard my ship in such an unceremonious manner, my worries have ceased entirely. Why? Because I shall need a mate on my return trip to Naples, Italy where I shall dispose of this schooner, for I am retiring from..."

Victor interrupted with, "That second mate of yours, Captain, is a *surly blighter.* I'm damn glad to hear that he will not return with us to Naples. As for the mate who came below—well, I don't get the drift of him, yet."

"You will understand both of them before we reach the slave coast," declared Captain Henry, significantly.

"I'm quite sure of that, sir," Victor chuckled.

Captain Henry and Victor went below again. Jud was grinning. He walked aft, tossing up his pocket knife. When alongside of Edith's open port, he dropped it. The man at the wheel did not notice the fact that Jud dropped a note through the port hole which said, "Victor is aboard. For God's sake, don't recognize him, Edith. He is known as Captain Simpson."

She had caught the note and glanced at it, tore it into pieces, then smiled. She had heard the deep, bass voice of Black Jack Barstow raging at Sir Henry. He had seen the little schooner pass on the beam, but had wondered at the name painted on her bow. She knew, instinctively, that the schooner was the Jenny that Captain Beasley had commanded back in Grimsby and wondered what had brought Victor Jenson aboard the Angel Girl at that moment, when she saw a man dive overboard and Black Jack had sent shot after shot at him. She smiled.

Edith came to the conclusion that her friends aboard the Jenny had some plan or other under way to free her from the bestial clutches of the man she now hated with the strength of despair. Believing so, she waited patiently for what might follow.

That night, she came face to face with Victor Jenson. The Countess Catherine Du Bois beamed at him. Edith frowned and turned her head aside, as Captain Henry said, smiling, "Ladies, I have the honor of presenting to you this evening, Captain Jack Simpson, of the coasting schooner "Lizzie Ann," who was, unfortunately, found drunk on the docks and shanghaied by that lubber of a captain aboard the Sea Ranger. Captain, meet the Countess Catherine Du Bois, chaperone to Lady Moresby's daughter, Edith Virginia Moresby, the great English prima donna, taking an ocean trip aboard my schooner for the benefit of her health before appearing at the opera house at Naples," he said, bowing to the ladies with courtly grace.

Victor bowed low and kissed the proffered hands of the ladies, but his face was a mask. However, in his eyes Edith read the deep concern he held for her safety aboard the "Angel Girl."

The steward announced that dinner was served.

Victor sat facing the countess. He smiled at her repeatedly. Soup, salads, vegetable, and fish were served, which fish much to the amazement of Captain Henry and Edith's friend Victor Jenson, she, apparently, enjoyed immensely. When they rose from the table that had been set with a great display of cut-glass, silver and gold plate, and the ladies were about to retire to their staterooms, Captain Henry gazed at Edith and commented, "That is the first time, my dear Edith, that I have seen you eat fish aboard of this schooner."

"Quite true, Sir Henry, but I have just learned to like it. It tastes delicious!" she smiled, as she cast a hurried glance at Victor, when Sir Henry turned to the sideboard and poured out a glass of wine. While doing so, the countess flashed her troubled gaze at the man she knew only as Captain Simpson and shook her head. "No, no!" it said. "Do not drink!" Victor understood. But for the countess, the trick he had carried aboard with him would have gone awry. Inwardly, he thanked her from his heart, as Captain Henry turned with glass in hand and handed it to Victor.

"Health and happiness to the ladies, sir!" he caught up his glass and raised it on high, then, dropping his monocle, as Vic replaced his glass upon the sideboard, said, "Why not, sir."

"That is what got me into trouble and made me lose my command and brought me aboard the "Angel Girl." No thank you!"

"I see," smiled Sir Henry, looking rather puzzledly from one to the other of the ladies. "But, Captain Simpson, something tells me that there is something fishy about the yarn you tell. If you are a navigator, sir, you cannot refuse to answer the questions I wish to ask you. If you can do so, well and good; if not, I shall know that you have lied to me. Perhaps you are one of the crew of those smugglers come aboard here for the purpose of sizing up the situation. At a given signal to those men of the Sea Ranger while my ship is anchored at the Bight, you would be raiding the Angel Girl of my gold and silver plate and the jewels you saw upon the lovely necks of the ladies; now retired to their staterooms. The penalty, sir, for having lied to the owner and commander of the Angel Girl will be detrimental to your health. You shall lie in chains below until I have wiped out of existence every one of those smugglers and sent their ship to the bottom. Then, I shall set you ashore in the jungles where you may find your way to the nearest port—if ever!"

Barkley glanced up the companionway to the deck above where Jud Beasley was standing. He saw him smiling grimly, as he sat down at the second table, waiting for Captain Henry to go up on deck and relieve Jud for dinner. He felt quite certain that Sir Henry suspected something afoot; who believed what would be attempted by the smugglers would not take place until he had anchored at the Bight. Even so, he felt quite safe, with the crew of the men for'ard who had served under his command on the Middle Passage.

Victor had smiled at Captain Henry's assertions and threats likewise.

Captain Henry and Victor went up on deck smoking. The former with his bull-dog pipe. The latter with a cigar that he had thrust into his pocket, telling Captain Henry that he only smoked on rising in the morning and five minutes before turning into his bunk at night. He had not the slightest doubt about it, but what that cigar, like the wine the countess had warned him not to drink, was doctored for the benefit of the noble Sir Henry who wanted his unwelcome guest to take a long, long sleep.

"Your questions, sir!" Victor suggested.

The monocle dropped from Sir Henry's eye. Those black, evil eyes of his glared at Victor, as he asked, "Captain Simpson, as a navigator, what would you do to find your longitude in cloudy weather, when for days, and possibly weeks at a time, you had not glimpsed the sun above you?"

Victor laughed. Jud and Beasley, with broad grins on their faces winked at each other as they sat at the table eating.

"You amuse me, sir!" Victor told Captain Henry. "I'd take an altitude at 11:45 am, then note the time of my watch and chronometer. Then I'd read altitude and take my meridian altitude for noon and clamp on altitude again and wait until it reached horizon. I would note the time by my watch and chronometer again, add the hours together, divide by two and apply my equation. Then, the difference between my watch and chronometer is my longitude in time. Can you or any other navigator beat that, sir?"

Sir Henry was smiling. He was satisfied, undoubtedly. His suspicious were allayed.

"'Pon my soul, I judged you wrongly, Captain. I offer you my sincere apology, sir. I shall sign you on as first mate of this schooner when we leave the gulf—homeward bound to Naples. Go below and turn in. My steward will show you your berth," he said, bowing to Victor.

A pair of grinning faces met him when he entered the cabin. Those grins were wiped off the faces of the two mates as the mulatto steward entered. He saw the two mates scowling at Victor and grinned, for he sensed the fact that the stranger was an unwelcome guest aboard the schooner.

He lost no time in communicating that fact to Captain Henry, who told him to watch the man. He did, but.....

23
VICTOR JENSON DISAPPEARS

❝This way, sir. I show you to your room," Selim had said, showing his white teeth in a broad grin.

Victor had nodded and trailed behind him. As the steward passed through the polished mahogany door that he had pushed open, leading to the for'ard part of the cabinet, the mates saw a door open a few inches and the hand of the countess thrust a note into the hands of Victor. Jud winked at Barkley, then muttered, "Imagine that, Jim!"

When Victor entered his stateroom and closed the door, he opened the note and read,

"Captain Simpson, I want to warn you. Do not drink anything, not even water, provided you by the steward. It will be drugged. I believe that Sir Henry suspects you to be other than what you represent yourself to be. Why, I do not know. Edith and I have talked over matters repeatedly. She refuses, absolutely, to consent to become his wife. She was tricked by her own mother into coming aboard this schooner at Gravesend. We are, I assure you, held prisoners aboard here. I myself and Lallah, my maid, have been his mistresses. We are, with Edith, doomed to enter the castle on the hill from which neither one of us will ever leave again in this life. The two mates are doomed to enter the jungles from which no man ever returns. Those who have incurred Sir Henry's displeasure have met with a horrible death in the jungle by the fangs of those two pet bloodhounds, Belial and Lucifer, that you must have seen for'ard.

"I firmly believe that you, yourself, will be set ashore with the two mates and disappear from human kind likewise. I beg of you to get in touch with them and try to do something to prevent Sir Henry from taking us girls to that castle of his on the hill at Assabah. Furthermore, I warn you that your every action will be watched by Selim, the mulatto steward. If he is not outside your door at this moment, listening in, or peeking through the keyhole of your door, then I do not know the man.

"Sir Henry contemplates boarding the schooner "Sea Ranger" and wiping out of existence every man aboard of her and setting fire to the schooner thereafter. He tells me we shall arrive at the Bight of the Niger next Sunday. You men must act quickly. Destroy this, if you value your life.

"Catherine Du Bois"

Victor laughed aloud. He did not destroy the note. He preserved it to hand to his friend Judson Beasley later. Trusting it in his pocket, he suddenly wrenched open his door and found the steward with his eye at the keyhole. He caught the mulatto by the nape of his neck and dragged him out through the for'ard entrance of the cabin to the quarter deck. There, he hit the steward a thundering whack on the jaw that bowled him over into the lee scuppers. There he lay yelping for Captain Henry.

The captain's response was to go for'ard to the break of the poop just as the two mates went up on deck. They saw him drop the monocle from his eye and gaze below.

"What's this?" Sir Henry blazed. "I thought you were sound asleep by this time, Simpson."

"I wanted a drink of water before turning in, sir. I opened my door and found that damn mulatto steward with his eye at the keyhole. The next time I catch him at that trick, I'll drag him out on deck and throw him overboard," Victor raged. The two mates, wiping the grins from their faces came for'ard to the break of the poop, scowling.

"Get below, you damn whelp when we arrive at the Bight." The steward understood his captain.

The steward slunk away into the cabin, muttering. Later, he went for'ard to his berth in the fore part of the galley where he, the cook, and the two caretakers of the dogs were domiciled.

Victor had returned to his room with a smile on his face. The first mate, likewise. Jud held the deck with the Captain. The rest of that night passed quietly. When Barkley relieved Judson Beasley at eight bells, midnight, the second mate, with a grin on his face, told Barkley that Victor refused to stay aboard the Angel Girl.

"My God, Jud, what do you mean by that?" Barkley whispered.

"Well, when Captain Henry went below and turned in, our old friend came up on deck and told me he did not appreciate the company aboard this schooner. And, would you believe it?" he burst out laughing, "he handed me that note the countess thrust into his hand when passing her door. I told him he was going man hunting in the jungles with us lubbers. He just up and told me, 'like hell I am!' They, Jim, were the last words he said as he dropped quietly overboard."

"He did? Good Lord! What, where, how in..."

"Cut that out, you lubber," Jud admonished.

"You told me he had a trick up his sleeve, and I wondered if it was the one you could outwit those of Sir Henry's, who has a hell of a lot of them to play with the help of his cutthroats for'ard there."

"Don't worry, Jim. He left his trick with me to play. And, you can bet your boots that hell will be popping on deck there for'ard before we reach port."

The wind, what little there was, had died out completely, long before Barkley and Victor had turned in that night. The haze on the gulf and the pitchy blackness of the night had swallowed up Victor Jenson. Jud went below and turned in, laughing like the devil. "Soon, but not yet!" he mumbled, as he closed his eyes in sleep, like a dog with one eye open.

24
JUST ONE DAMN FOOL LESS

After breakfast, when the mates went up on deck, Captain Henry informed them that his guest had not slept in his berth that night. They both stared at him amazed. He turned to them and asked if they had seen the lubber come up on deck during their watch. They lied without hesitation.

"No sir! If he did so, he made himself invisible, I guess, sir," Jud remarked, "That lubber sensed the fact that the mate and I considered him doubly unwelcome aboard this ship. I believe, sir, that he is hiding out on us in some part of the schooner; if not, then he must have jumped overboard. I had an idea that fellow was crazy, believe me, sir."

"Search the ship," the captain thundered. "The man acted as though he was insane last night. I felt that there was something wrong." He scowled at the mates as they went for'ard to search for the man who was God only knew where, thought Barkley, at that moment. As he gazed around the gulf, there was no sign of the "Sea Ranger" in sight. North, hugging the land, were a few coasting luggers.

The only place one could search was down in the forepeak. The lazarette was padlocked and the key in possession of Captain Henry. Not once, since the mate had shipped aboard the schooner had he been permitted to glimpse therein. What Sir Henry kept secreted there was known only to him and the countess. He had told Jud about it and the latter had hinted he would find out from the countess, if possible, what Sir Henry had hid in that hole. If he had done so, he had not communicated his discovery to the mate.

They went down to the chain locker, for'ard, where the cook kept his coat for the galley. Abaft of it was a lot of old sails and tarry rope. Jud remarked, "He ain't here, Jim."

The mate raised his lantern up to Jud's face. He was grinning. "Stop funning," he grouched.

"Be careful of that pipe of yours, Jim. A spark from it will set fire to that junk and oakum in the twinkling of an eye. A nice bonfire it would make! Once ablaze, nothing could save this ship from destruction. But say, Jim, what is in the hold below deck?" he asked.

"Just ballast; unsinkable lumber, stores, and ammunition, I daresay. In the fore part of the cabin there is a cubby hole leading into the store rooms that only the steward enters. They may be entered down the hold, amidships. One of them contains a hell of a lot of ammunition, guns, cutlasses and.....well, what of it? We can't get at them, anyway."

They went aft with a dubious look on their faces and faced Captain Henry.

"Find that unexpected guest of mine?" asked Sir Henry.

Jud shook his head. Barkley suggested, "Jumped overboard, sir. But he certainly did not..."

Captain Henry interrupted him and blazed, "Just one damn fool less!"

He went below and left the mates grinning at each other.

The schooner Angel Girl was rolling, lazily, from port to starboard, starboard to port, while her sails slattered out with whip-like cracks against the starboard rigging. They hauled the sheets in, took a pull on the throat and peak halyards of the big sails and, with the perspiration streaming down their faces, stood on the break of the poop glancing around the gulf through their binoculars. There was no wind to keep headway on the schooner. She was heading all points of the compass and drifting with the tide out to sea.

It was some hellish trip that, for the two mates, especially for Barkley who was waiting day by day for something to happen. But Jud kept on smiling. Barkley believed that his friend, Judson Beasley, would be smiling if the schooner was on fire or sinking under him. Not once, all that day, through the terrific heat and haze of the gulf did he appear to be the least concerned about the future. The schooner was right on the equator at that time and seemed to be standing still upon it, but she was nevertheless drifting westward out of the Gulf of Guinea, but she would drift back on the flood tide.

That night, during the dog-watch hour, between six and eight o'clock, the two Negroes had the dogs out on deck and the whole crew up in the rigging. It was laughable to see the looks upon the faces of those men who had, undoubtedly, fought many a bloody battle side by side aboard the old Spitfire and other ships they had boarded on the high seas. Shot and shell and cold steel never made them jump around so quickly as those two ferocious bloodhounds did. The mates stood on the poop laughing at them. One of the blighters yelled, "You laugh now, Mr. Barkley, and you—you Yankee pig, but by and by we laugh at you. We safe aboard the schooner. Soon, we say goodbye to you both; we see you no more. We go to Naples and have a good time ashore there—after we get paid off."

"Like hell you will!" Jud barked at them. "When Jim and I get ashore after we kill them damn dogs in the jungle, we shall come aboard and take you all back to England where you will get your necks stretched good and plenty. You are all wanted there and you know it. Not one of you ever dared to go ashore at Gravesend.

"Hey there, you black imps of the devil!" yelled Jud at the caretakers of the dogs, "get after that lubber I licked on the passage down. Can't you see him on the fo'c'sle deck hiding behind that gun? Keep them dogs moving. What's the matter with them? Chase the lubber over the bow; if you don't, I'll report you both to the captain for neglecting your duty."

The two blacks grinned and the dogs, under leash, began to climb up to the fo'c'sle deck. The bully of the fo'c'sle ran to the bow and climbed out to the far end of the jib-boom. There he sat perched, scowling, and cursing back at the mates, while the men up in the rigging out of reach of the dogs every man hated, laughed aloud.

The mates expected to see Sir Henry come up on deck. He did not. He was with the countess, they thought. But they were mistaken, for as they went aft, passing by the open port window of the Belle of Grimsby, they heard him talking with her.

Later, he came up on deck as the sun went down beyond the horizon west of them with the two ladies. He glanced for'ard and laughed, "Just look at those two pets of mine, Edith. Poor things, cooped up in their kennels, day after day, in this sweltering heat. But it won't be long now before they get liberty ashore for a few days," he announced, ironically, glancing at his two mates with a devilish grin on his face.

"How like you they are, Sir Henry!" Lady Moresby's daughter said. "what did you say their names are?

"Belial and Lucifer," he replied, smiling, but the next moment he stood scowling at her for Edith remarked, "Imps of the devil, their master and owner."

"Go below to your room," he commanded, as he turned to the mates and told them to set all sail again.

"All hands on deck!" barked the second mate as he went for'ard, while Edith told Sir Henry that nothing could please her better than to be rid of his hateful presence.

The countess followed her. Below they conversed in whispers a moment or so before they entered their rooms. The steward, on watch, crept toward the door of the Belle of Grimsby and locked it, thrusting the key back into his pocket, then tiptoed out of the cabin back to the galley.

Suddenly, as is usual down on the equator with the setting sun, darkness fell upon the water of the gulf. A pitchy blackness and the steaming haze enveloped the schooner. Captain Henry held the deck aft until four bells, 10:00 pm and being quite satisfied that his watch dogs were for'ard, his cutthroat crew were ever on the watch, he went below to the room of the countess with a sardonic grin upon his face.

When Barkley relieved Jud at eight bells, midnight, the second mate whispered, "It won't be long now, Jim. Keep a good lookout to port. We are just below the equator. The little breeze died out an hour ago. We are drifting in with the tide, however, toward Annobon Island. I'm not sleeping a wink this watch."

"It won't be long for what?" the mate asked.

"Before hell breaks loose!" Beasley answered, grimly.

25
A LIGHT ON THE PORT BEAM

At four bells, 2:00 am, the darkness on the gulf was intense. Edith's retort had inspired Sir Henry to set all sail upon the schooner with the exception of the flying-jib that Jimmy Grimes, a naval reserve gunner aboard the schooner Jenny had brought down.

The big sails of the schooner were flapping back and forth and the chug, chug of the sheet-blocks abaft the helmsman got on Barkley's nerves. He wondered how any one below in the cabin could sleep that night. All was as silent as the grave, otherwise. He felt inwardly that something was going to happen aboard the schooner before the sun rose again over the distant mountains. What, he could not then imagine.

He went for'ard to the break of the poop and stood gazing through his binoculars around the gulf. The man on the lookout and leaning against the gun carriage was probably asleep at the time, he thought.

He had a notion of going for'ard to see where the watch on deck was. He was about to descend to the main deck when he heard the door to the for'ard entrance to the cabin creak. He thought it might be the mulatto steward and waited. A moment later, he saw Jud stick his head out and gaze up at him.

"See any light on the port beam?" he asked Barkley, in a whisper.

"No!" he said, as he raised his glasses again and stared through them, then lowered them again.

The helmsman had the wheel in the becket. He stood lolling against it, dozing. He was thirty feet or more aft from where the mate stood and could not hear the mates whispering. He could not see Jud on the quarter deck. He said, "Listen, Jim. That little breeze while I was up on deck was a godsend. If the Jenny is not hove to, a few cables length away, I miss my guess. Her sails, unlike the white canvass aboard this schooner, blend in with the steaming haze on the gulf, making her invisible in this pitchy blackness. No lights showing, as we have aboard here."

"Before you came up on deck, I saw a signal from her. I expected it and was watching out sharply for it."

"What signal, Jud?"

"One that Victor and I had agreed upon before he slipped quietly overboard, you lubber!"

"How in hell did he get back aboard the schooner?"

"A boat from the Jenny was trailing us at the appointed time and picked him up. Get that?"

"I do, but I don't get the drift of..."

"Cut that out, Jim," Jud interrupted. "Captain Henry, feeling secure since his guest went overboard, celebrated the event after I had all sail upon the schooner with the exception of the flying-jib and went below to the room of the countess and got drunk. I saw the steward taking brandy and champagne into the room of the countess. Lallah told me he was drunk and the countess likewise. But, I guess that when hell breaks loose aboard here he will be up on deck in a jiffy...here, take this," he whispered, handing Barkley a cutlass.

"Where did you get that?"

"I borrowed the keys from the mulatto steward, who is sleeping like a baby—maybe," he grinned. Then, seriously, "If that black devil of hell comes up on deck, crack him on the head with it. Failing to do so, he will shoot hell out of you!" he warned, as he slunk for'ard on the lee side of the deck in the darkness on all fours.

Barkley stood in the alley way, aft, between the cabin and the rail with the cutlass in his hand out of sight of the man at the wheel, wondering where in hell Jud had gone. He came back shortly and whispered, "Every lubber for'ard down below except the man on the lookout is asleep at the switch."

"Listen. I have that damn steward bound hand and foot and gagged in my bunk. He can't move or talk until I want him to. But the silence down in the cabin is frightful. I stumbled over that black cat, Satan, and gave him a kick and sent him up on deck. See him?" he asked.

"No, Jud."

"Look, Jim!" he whispered, pointing to a light that suddenly flared up on the port beam.

"What's that?" Barkley asked, stupidly.

"The signal, you lubber! Go aft again and stand by to give the devil his due. He has got it coming, right now! The time is ripe to play the trick I've had up my sleeve for ages, so it seems. Go aft!" he commanded, as he himself slunk for'ard again, telling himself the mate was too damn nervous.

Barkley gazed for'ard and saw the watch on deck standing by the port rail, watching the light. Two or three of the men were up in the rigging on the weather side of the ship gazing at it as the man on the lookout reported the light.

"Aye, aye! Keep your eyes on it, me hearties," Jim replied, as he watched Jud on the lee side disappear from view.

He wondered what Jud was up to, but he kept his eyes on the light, the men for'ard and on the companion-hatch, expecting to see Sir Henry at any moment. His eyes were everywhere. He had to confess to himself he was exceedingly nervous at the moment. Any blighter, he thought placed as he was at that moment between the devil and hell knew what, who said he was not so, would be a blasted liar. His nerves were tense. He breathed hard. He thought of his fate in the jungle, along with his friend, if the schooner arrived there. He felt his heart thumping his throat, as he grasped the cutlass ready to drop Sir Henry to the deck and then settle with the helmsman likewise.

The light on the beam flickered out for a moment and he saw the watch about to leave the rail.

"Stand by and watch that blasted light, you lubbers! See what you can make of it, me hearties," he yelled at them, as he watched for the appearance of Sir Henry.

"By God!" he muttered inwardly, "he must be damned drunk not to hear me yelling like that."

He gazed for'ard, just a fleeting glance, and saw all the watch at the weather side of the ship gazing out on the gulf. But in that quickening glance, he saw Jud crawling aft on all fours in the lee scuppers. He breathed a sigh of relief. Here he was, mate of the schooner, and had been taking orders from his second mate all down the coast to the gulf. A grin spread over his face thinking about it. He wondered now what command he would get from Judson Beasley, as the second mate climbed up on the poop, stretching himself and yawning as though he had just tumbled out of his bunk.

He stood yawning alongside of the mate, aft, while the helmsman, now wide awake, glared at them. Jud commented, "I'll be damned if I could sleep, Jim. But say, what is that light on the port beam?"

"I daresay it was some lugger on fire, but I think they have got it under way," Barkley replied.

Not a movement in the cabin below decks. They wondered. Jud whispered, as she moved for'ard a bit, "Captain Henry?"

"Must be dead drunk. If he were not so, Jud, he or I would be a corpse by this time."

They went aft again and glanced at the binnacle.

"What do you know about that?" Jud asked, gazing down the companionway. "The schooner is heading due west. Say you," he barked at the helmsman, "stick that wheel in the becket and go for'ard and take a smoke and turn in."

"Aye, aye, sir! I appreciate that—Gawd blimey I do," the man chuckled as he slouched away for'ard.

"Maybe not! Every one will be smoking like hell, shortly," Jud threw after him.

"What did you do for'ard, Jud?"

"Just set a little hell raging down the fore-peak. That stuff down there was touchable. Look for'ard now," he suggested, as he took the cutlass from the mate and went below.

Barkley, minus the cutlass, went to the rail and grasped up an iron belaying pin, then gazed for'ard. He saw the black forms of men rushing out of the fo'c'sle, yelling, "Fire, fire, fire!"

Barkley, with a grin on his face, roared back, "Pass the buckets, you lubbers. I'll call Captain Henry up on deck."

He stood on the starboard side of the hatchway with the belaying pin resting on his shoulder and the men for'ard heard him yelling, "Captain Henry!.....Captain Henry! Rouse out of it and shake a leg down there. The schooner is on fire!"

But there was no response. He wondered what had become of Judson Beasley, for all was silent below decks.

26
SONS OF THE SEA

The two bosuns had the men busy with the buckets, trying to put out the flames that seethed up out of the open hatch of the fore-speak. Barkley knew that their efforts were useless; that the coal had caught fire and was eating its way through the bulkhead into the cargo of lumber between deck.

While he stood at the companionway on guard, waiting for the appearance of Captain Henry, Jud rushed out of the for'ard entrance of the cabin and sprang up on the poop deck, ran aft to Barkley and handed him his cutlass, brandishing one in his right hand while telling the mate to hold the deck there. He believed Barkley would be useless in a fight on deck.

"I'll hold them cutthroats back from the poop until Black Jack Barstow, Victor, and his men, sons of the sea, board us. Should be here right now," he bawled, as he rushed for'ard and dropped to the quarter deck.

The helmsman Jud had sent for'ard to get a smoke had told the bosun of his watch that he believed the second mate had started the fire. With a howl of rage, he yelled at the men to drop their buckets and get their weapons out of the fo'c'sle before it was too late. Armed with cutlasses, pikes, and long dirks, they went aft yelling like madmen.

"Come on, you mongrel curs," Jud barked at them, as he heard a bumping noise alongside of the schooner. I told you lubbers that you would not land in Naples. I'm sending you all to hell where you belong, where you'll be smoking, shortly. Take that and that and that!" he laughed, as three of the crew dropped to the deck groaning.

The clash of steel met steel as black forms climbed aboard the schooner. Howls of rage met Barkley's ears as the fishermen of Grimsby, all sons of the sea, led by Black Jack and Victor, pressed the maddened curs, inch by inch, back for'ard.

The foresail had now caught fire. The light flared on the faces of the grim fishermen and the hearts of the cutthroats quailed, as they gave way repeatedly before them. The fishermen cut and slashed away at the ruffians who outnumbered them two to one. Groans of agony from them and the maddened laughter from the second mate reached Barkley, but he could not see the carnage down on the quarter deck.

Wondering at the silence below in the cabin, he ran down the companionway to see what was what, for his inaction had almost unnerved him. He could no longer stand the strain.

He stepped across the cabin as the light in the gimbals was about to go out, he thought. He saw Lallah, the maid of the countess, stagger out from the countess's room and drop to the cabin floor outside it.

"Good God!" he muttered, stooping down by her side. "What is this?" he asked, while out on deck he heard the clashing of steel against steel and the curses of men fighting for their lives.

The graceful creature was dying. She pointed to Edith's door then muttered, "Captain Henry gave Edith a sleeping powder, as she said she had a headache. He and countess drunk. He gave her drugged wine, then made me drink. I spit out some. I go to room where I had knife I go back to countess room and see him in her arms. I stick knife in his back. He die. Lallah no care. I die, too. Save Edith," she said, pointing again at her door. The next moment she died in Barkley's arms.

Lifting her graceful form in his arms from the deck, he placed her on a couch and went to Edith's door. The howls of Belial and Lucifer became silent as the foremast went over with a thundering crash, the galley and dog kennels crashing into the seething furnace below.

Edith's door was locked. He went to the captain's stateroom for an axe he knew was hanging therein along with swords and cutlasses, then ran out and glanced into the room of the countess. He saw Captain Henry sprawled out on the Persian rug with a long dirk sticking in his back. He glanced at the almost nude form of the countess. A smile was on her lovely face and her eyes were wide open; but she was dead. He was horror-stricken. He backed away with the axe in hand and crashed in the door of Edith's stateroom, when he heard Jud Beasley bawling at the remnants of the crew of ruffians, "Get that long boat over the side, while you have a chance. Get into it! If the rest of you mongrels can reach Annobon Island, you may remain there to become food for the alligators that infest the swamps there."

Less than one third of the crew of the Angel Girl got into the boat, some of them wounded, as they pulled away from the burning schooner that had now become a roaring furnace. The mainsail caught fire. Jud and Victor, with cutlasses in hand stained with the blood of the cutthroats, burst into the cabin, as Barkley was trying to awaken Edith.

Pushing the mate aside, Jud caught up the lovely girl in his arms and carried her up the companionway to the deck where some of the fishermen stood by to lower the captain's gig. The mate and Victor had followed him in silence.

"Get into the boat, my friends," Jud commanded.

He handed Edith to his friend Victor, then told the men to lower away. Black Jack and his men were in the boat from the schooner Jenny, waiting for Judson Beasley. He yelled, "Jud, come on, you lubber!"

"Wait, Jack. I can't let that steward roast alive in hell. I'll be back in a jiffy. I have him bound and gagged in my bunk. Captain Henry and the countess and her maid is dead. The black devil drugged them, but Lallah knifed him in the back.

The next moment, Jud disappeared again. The main mast was burning furiously. Black Jack yelled again for Jud, telling him the schooner would go to the bottom with him. Jud came up on deck laughing, with Satan, the black cat in his arms.

"There's your course, damn you!" he said, as he threw the cat overboard. "May you land in the stomach of a shark or an alligator, if you can reach that Island." The next moment he disappeared below again. The steward was dead.

"My God!" exclaimed Black Jack Barstow. "Let me get aboard and yank that damn mad Yankee out of this hell."

He was about to board the schooner when he saw Jud peering down at him. "Stand by to get this sea chest of mine, Jack," he said, with a broad grin on his face.

"My God, men! Risking his life for a lousy sea chest," he grouched, as he caught the chest into the boat and cast off the sling. The next moment Jud went down the falls astern into the Captain's gig and told the two men to sheer off.

A cable's length away, the schooner Jenny loomed up before them. The light from the doomed schooner-yacht glared into the faces of the men who stood at the rail as the two boats pulled toward them.

Barkley was asking, "What was that light that loomed up on the port beam, a half hour before you boarded us, Victor?"

"The signal that Jud and I agreed upon. That we were coming to board the Jenny. Jud said that we would be needing a light aboard the Angel Girl, but I had no idea that he meant to set fire to the schooner. He sure made some light," he laughed.

"I did that, Victor. I had gambled on that, to scare the liver out of them ruffians. Steel in front of them with fire roasting their backs did the trick. But look!" he suggested, with a grin on his face as he held Edith close to his breast, kissing her, hoping to awaken her. "There goes the Angel Girl, bow first, to the bottom of the gulf, right on top of the lugger, Mary Jane—maybe!"

With a roaring, seething, hissing, boiling noise, the Angel Girl, with its gruesome cargo on the quarter deck and the eternally dead in the cabinet, disappeared from human kind.

When they boarded the Jenny as Judson Beasley carried the lovely form of the Belle of Grimsby below, Black Jack Barstow commented, "That was a good job well done, Jud."

"It was, Jack, but it is not yet finished," Beasley said, grimly.

His three friends stared at him, then at each other. Barstow grouched, "Not finished? Has he gone daft, Victor?"

"I daresay not!" Victor laughed.

Constantinople
Constantinople was the capital of the Eastern Roman Empire now
Istanbul; the largest city of Turkey.

27
JUD BEASLEY'S SEA CHEST

The bosun, Bill Blake, who was mate of the Porpoise, one of Black
Jack Barstow's fishing schooners, had given first aid to the five
wounded fishermen and sent them aft to the cabin. Jud reluctantly left
Edith to attend to them, after placing her in the captain's stateroom
berth. He had tried repeatedly to awaken her, but time alone would
bring her out of her stupor.

When the men went for'ard, they told their mates that for every
drop of blood they had lost in the fight, Captain Beasley was going to
add a quid to their wages upon their arrival back in Grimsby. The
bosun grouched, "By God! If there's goin' to be any more fighting,
mates, I aim to get into it. Damn it! Me and Jimmy Grimes were chief
gunner's mates aboard Her Majesty's ship Scorpion that run a slaver
into the gulf here a few years ago. Me, the champion bruiser of the
British Navy left aboard the Jenny to navigate her back to Grimsby in
case them four lubbers back there kicked the bucket. Hell! I got to lick
somebody before we get back home!"

Tom Lawler, a brawny fisherman, with a mop of red hair, red face,
and twinkling blue eyes, spouted, "Try to lick any of us lubbers, Bill,
and we'll jump you. You couldn't lick the late Captain Robert Boyd and
if you ever run up against our Yankee skipper's fist—well," he grinned,
"you'd go to sleep like a baby."

"Boyd had no conscience, you lubber! All he did to me was grab me
around the waist and try to break my back. That was no fair fight, but I

sure don't want to run afoul of Captain Beasley," he concluded with a broad grin on his pugilistic looking face.

Roars of laughter followed his assertion as Jud Beasley joined his three friends up on deck where they stood conversing as the Jenny headed in toward the slave coast.

"That sea chest, Jud. What is in it?" asked Barstow.

"Come below. I'll show you. Maybe just a lot of junk!"

Below in the cabin he took a large key from his pocket—one such that his friends had never seen the like of in their lives. He gazed at them a moment with gleaming eyes as he twirled around his finger a large ring that Barkley had seen upon Sir Henry's finger. He gazed at it a moment, then informed them, "The countess told me while I was in her room that night, Jim, that in the lazarette was a chest that contain…Well, she said, when he was drunk, he had told her there was more than a million pounds in it. She said that I should not fail to take it along with us, when, if ever, we returned to England. I was remindful of it at the last minute."

"You believed her, I daresay?" Barkley said, sarcastically.

"I did you lubber! Now," he smiled sadly, thinking of the lovely woman's end, "we shall see if she lied to me. She told me he had procured from it the necklace she wore and those jewels he had forced upon Edith. That necklace alone would bring ten thousand pounds or more in London."

He turned the key in the lock, massive affair it was, and, before throwing up the lid gazed at his friends. "Now get ready to laugh at me for risking my life for a sea chest full of junk," he said, as he calmly threw up the lid.

Black Jack and Barkley fell back gasping. Victor stood staring at the contents like a man entranced. Barstow was the first to recover his speech. "What are you going to do with it, Jud?" he said.

Beasley stooped and picked out a necklace. "I dare venture to assume that is the mate to the one Edith has. It shall be a wedding present to Victor's sister, Jenny, when she marries a lubber named Black Jack Barstow," Jud declared, then added, "But she has got to have the rest of the fixings to go with this lovely, pearl necklace. Just look at that, Victor! Wouldn't that look stunning around her lovely neck?"

Not one of his friends could speak. They merely nodded, as he went on, "There are several tiaras studded with over a hundred one, two, and three carat diamonds, pigeon-blood rubies and emeralds. Rings and bracelets to match and there are in these chamois skin bags, count them: over a dozen more than five hundred loose diamonds, rubies, emeralds and pearls, all of the best quality. Each one contains a king's ransom, so what!"

He closed down the lid then asked Victor to help him store the chest away in the lazarette.

"That wealth, Jack, will be divided between all hands on this ship. One fifth to the sons of the sea for'ard and the rest between us four lubbers. Your share alone, Jack, will enable you to buy out the Sanderson Brothers' fleet and build a half dozen or more schooners like the "Jenny." There is no question about that. The countess told me that Sir Henry was selling jewels on every trip to London, Naples, Paris, and Constantinople and that his wealth was apparently inexhaustible. So you see that the poor, unfortunate creature told me the truth. Let us go up on deck," he suggested, after glancing into the room occupied by Edith. "She will surely awaken shortly."

A little breeze in the offing brought a smile to his face. "I told you, Jack, that my work was not finished. I mean just that," he said. "As captain and owner of this schooner, you and Victor are passenger. Jim Barkley is mate until we reach Grimsby. Then the Jenny will be turned over to her new owner, Captain Victor Jenson, who resigned his command to sail under a bean-eater from Boston as my mate. Satisfied?"

"No, by God! I object to risking my men's lives again, Jud."

"How about you two lubbers?" Jud asked, turning to Victor and Barkley.

"With you to the finish!" they declared.'

"Your objections are over-ruled, Jack. Another word out of you and I'll clap you in irons. Get me?" he asked, winking at the mate and Victor.

They nodded. Black Jack grouched, "I do, but where in hell are you bound, now?"

"To the castle on the hill at Assabah. The countess told me that Sir Henry's father did not die of the sleeping sickness in the jungles. He lives there and I suspect that he is no other than Captain Mort of the Spitfire who hung my father to the yard arm of his ship. I want his head! I want to hang that bloody slaver to the peak of my main sail; then, I am finished."

"Take it from me, Jud, if we land there on the slave coast, hell will be popping again. Some of us may not live to return to Grimsby," said Black Jack, still convinced that since they had rescued the Belle of Grimsby from the clutches of that black devil, Sir Henry, the safest course for all hands would be to head back to Grimsby.

Jud laughed, "I shall enter that castle alone. Neither you, Victor, nor Barkley, nor yet any of my men—I said my men," this with a smile at Jack, "since I am paying their wages and not you, need to risk their necks ashore there. By hook or by crook Jack, I shall enter the castle with the key that will open the gates for me and bring Captain Mort back to my ship, or else..."

Jud grinned at Barkley. "Take a pull on the halyards, Jim. Lift up the throat and peek of fore and main."

"Aye, aye, sir!" Barkley replied, going for'ard to the break of the poop and passing the word along to Bill Blake, the bosun, as Black Jack muttered, "Or else, what, Jud?"

"Well, there is a possibility, of course, that I may fail to convince Captain Mort and that I may be detained there ever after."

"Like hell you will! In that case, I'll come ashore with my men and raise a doubly, damned hell there and yank you out of that castle and Captain Mort. Victor and I when at school, before we boarded our father's ships to go fishing up in the North Sea studying navigation, read about the exploits of Black Mort on the Middle Passage and both of us wished we could get on a slaver and meet that devil face to face. Victor and I never served in the navy, but take it from me that we both know how to handle a sword."

"I know damn well you both can handle a cutlass," Jud said, grinning at them, thinking of their actions aboard the schooner Angel Girl at that moment. "As I said before, you are not now a member of my crew, but a friend and passenger. No matter what happens to me, you will stay aboard this ship. Victor," he said, turning to the man he loved as a brother, "I am a fatalist and firmly believe I shall accomplish my object on the coast there and return with you to Grimsby—when my work is done. Come for'ard with me," he commanded his two friends.

He stood with gleaming eyes watching the fishermen at their work by the side of Barkley. When the ropes were belayed and all shipshape again, he yelled, "All hands lay aft!"

The bosun blew his whistle and repeated the order. When the men stood on the quarter deck gazing up at the four friends, Jud spouted, "Sons of the sea, all fishermen born, I want to tell you that I am heading to the slave coast and that it is my intention to enter the castle there on the hill, a little north of the Bight of the Niger, and bring Captain Mort, that piratical slaver most of you men read about in the years gone by, aboard my ship and hang him to the peak of my main sail. Why? He is the man who destroyed my father's ship, the "Fanny Rawlings," killed the crew, then hung my father to the yard arm of his ship, the Spitfire whose skeletal remains rest there at the Bight of the Niger. I own this ship. I am paying you all double wages. Upon our return to Grimsby, I want to assure you all that every jack man of you will be rich enough to purchase a couple of schooners like this and then some. Can I foot that bill, Jack?' he asked, turning to Black Jack Barstow with a smile on his handsome face, his eyes shining like the precious emeralds he had brought aboard.

"He can, men. He could buy out the Barstow and Sanderson's fleet and build a half dozen more like them," he declared.

The men stood grinning at each other as Jud went on, "I have not the slightest doubt about it, men, that I am running a great risk but assure you in that case, there may be more fighting to do before we return to Grimsby from the slave coast. Now if there is a lubber among you who object to raising hell ashore there, if necessary, step over to starboard. That man or men will remain aboard ship and receive his bonus just the same shortly after we arrive in Grimsby—if ever!" he ended.

Every man, still grinning, stood perfectly still. The bosun glanced up at Captain Beasley and bawled, "Every bloomin' lubber of us are with you to the end, Captain. We'll follow you clean plumb into hell and back!"

"Grog ho! I thank you all!" Jud said calmly, as the men roared, "Three cheers for our Yankee Skipper!"

When their voices subsided, Jud turned to his friends. "Come below, my friends. We have to go to talk over things."

When Jud stepped into the cabin and peeked into Edith's room, he found her seated there, staring around her dazedly.

"Where are we, Jud?" she asked, smiling wanly, and glancing at Victor, Black Jack and Barkley, questioningly.

"Aboard the schooner Jenny, darling; Captain Judson Beasley in command," he assured her, longing to take her in his arms.

"I do not understand, Jud. Where is Sir Henry and the countess. Are they safe?"

"Absolutely!" exclaimed Jud, glancing at his friends.

"But where are they?"

"Aboard the Angel Girl, he informed her grimly.

Bight of the Niger
The Bight of Bonny is located off the West African coast in the
easternmost part of the Gulf of Guinea. It extends from the river delta
of the Niger in the north.

28
STAND BY THE LONG BOAT

The sun rose over the distant mountains of the slave coast as the
schooner cut through the rippling waters of the gulf. A little five
knot breeze on the port beam drove her steadily along, while the watch
on deck, inspired by Bill Blake the bosun, were squatted there
sharpening their cutlasses. Jud was watching them with a grim smile on
his face.

"Every man of them are anxious for a fight. I am hopeful of
disappointing them. I have not the slightest doubt about it, my friends,
that I shall be successful in tricking Black Mort into coming aboard my
schooner. Then what?

"I'd clap him in irons and head back to Grimsby; but, mates, not
with that lubber aboard. He shall pay the extreme penalty he so richly
deserves," he assured them as the steward announced breakfast was
served.

Subsequently, the third night after the Angel Girl went to the
bottom of the gulf, the schooner Jenny glided like a swan into a cove
north of the castle on the hill, out of sight of its occupants and the
stockades likewise. The jibs and stay sails and main gaff topsail were
hauled down as the anchor was dropped into six fathoms of water.

The fore and main sail were left standing. The sheets were hauled in
amidships and booms guyed. The throat and peak of both sails were
lifted up, stretching both sails taut. There they flexed gently in the off-

shore breeze ready for a quick get away, if necessary. Then he commanded, "Stand by the long boat!"

The long boat was launched quietly. Judson Beasley picked out his boat's crew, calling them by name. Bill Blake, Jimmy Grimes, Tom Lawler, David MacDonald, Jerry Morgan, and Pat McShane, all brawny fishermen – fishermen born, who loved nothing better than a good fight.

The rest of the crew, counting the five wounded men who, while able to do their bit aboard the schooner to lend a hand, one hand only, were naturally unable to wield a cutlass. The other six men, ready to go to hell and back again for Captain Beasley, stood at the rail gazing down on the boat's crew telling them they were damned lucky.

Bill Blake, the bosun, said they might be damned glad that they were not called. One of them remarked, "If there is to be any fighting, Bill, and you don't come back for us lubbers, when you come aboard, if you live to do so, we will knock hell out of you. Got to lick somebody before we land in Grimsby and you will be it."

"Maybe, but don't worry, mates. If there is any chance of a fight ashore, you blokes will be in it. You can gamble on that, me hearties."

Smiles wreathed the faces of the fishermen aboard the schooner as they waited to see their captain push off on an adventure that no man knew the ending of.

Captain Beasley was conversing with his friends on the break of the poop, away from Edith's open port window. He was telling Barkley, the mate, that he would find secret orders in his desk if things went awry and he was detained in the castle. Otherwise, he would be bringing Captain Mort aboard the schooner by 2:00 am; four bells. Jack grinned and said he if was not back by five bells, he and the rest of the crew would be entering the castle and yank him and Black Mort out of it.

Captain Beasley informed him and Victor, pointedly, that they were guests aboard and he did not want them to take any such chances. Victor's mother and sister would be needing him and Jack's mother likewise. Both of his friends nodded, as much as to say, you are right about that, Jud, but....

Jud told them that in his desk were letters and papers addressed to both of them—that Barkley would hand them over upon their arrival in Grimsby and not before.

"Damn careful," I should say, blurted Black Jack. "Here we have Edith aboard, safe and sound, and, by God, Jud, there is no reason whatever for you to thrust your neck into that den of evil ashore. Hell, you don't know what you may run up against!" he blazed.

"Of course not, Jack. I realize that fact. My work is not finished as long as Captain Mort lives. Edith's silence and the article I read in the paper that you tell me you saw in the London Telegraph sent me in quest of the devil and down here into the gulf. Not even my love for her can stop me now. It was fated for me to wipe out of existence that damned, piratical slaver. When I do a job—when I tackle anything—I finish it," he declared vehemently.

He told them to hold the deck; that he was going below to dress and inform Edith of his departure. His eyes were gleaming as he left them, but after dressing and buckling on a jeweled, hilted sword that he had taken from the late Captain Henry's berth at the last moment, he stood a moment twirling the massive ring around his finger, smiling grimly at it, before he rapped upon Edith's door.

Edith's melodious voice called, "Come!"

He entered smiling, bowing to the girl, wondering if he dared to take her in his arms that night

He stood before her, waiting for her to speak. She was reclining on a couch and had been reading a book. She smiled up at him, then asked, "Well, Jud, why the sword?"

"I am going ashore, Edith. I have a very important message to deliver to Sir Henry's father who resides in the castle on the hill. I wanted to say au revoir, but not goodbye," he said, smiling at her with the love light in his eyes as he stood twirling the ring around his finger.

Edith glanced at the ring. She recognized it immediately.

"This," he assured her, is the key that will unlock the gate of the castle for me. I see you recognize it, my dear. Yes, it came from your friend, the devil. It is one that will introduce me to that blasted, piratical slaver, Captain Mort of the Spitfire, the man who hung my father to the yard arm of his ship."

Edith sensed the fact at that moment that the man she loved was on a vengeance bent. She frowned at him.

"Jud, dear, if you love me, do something for me, please." She was sobbing now. He waited. She went on, "I want you to remain aboard and set sail immediately for Grimsby."

"Sorry I cannot consider your gentle request at this time, Edith. Your silence and the article in the London Telegraph sent me in quest of the devil and brought me down here into the Gulf of Guinea. When my work is finished, I shall return to Grimsby and not before. Again, I say I am sorry, my darling," he said gently, as he stooped over her, held her close and kissed her passionately upon her ripe, red lips. Edith struggled free and flared at him, "My silence. How dare you say…."

He bowed with gentlemanly grace as he interrupted her, "Yes, your silence. Goodnight!"

He turned on his heel and was about to close the door when Edith asked, "Are there girls ashore at the castle?"

"Oh yes, Edith; lovely girls, I assure you," he threw back at her, stood a moment waiting, then closed her door and ran up the companionway to the deck.

Edith wanted to scream. She wanted to call him back. She wanted to call him back and ask him why he accused her of being silent and what he meant by the article he had read in a London paper; but pride and her stubborn disposition prevented. She dropped back on her couch and began sobbing bitterly and before she went to sleep that night, she decided not to refer to the subject again.

Notwithstanding the fact that the countess had written him declaring that Edith refused to marry Sir Henry, he did not believe her. Had he not heard the late Captain Henry telling Edith that when the countess entered the castle on the hill, in accordance with her own desire, he would set sail for Naples and dispose of the schooner and there, at the Villa Rosa, await the coming of Lady Moresby before they were married. He had not heard Edith's objection to such an arrangement on that day. She had fallen to sobbing gently and he had misconstrued her silence, believing she had merely nodded assent.

He had prevented Sir Henry from carrying out his plans and, grimly told himself, that after he had finished his work on the slave coast, he would have the pleasure of returning the Belle of Grimsby to her mother, Lady Moresby, and of informing her personally of Sir Henry's demise. A fire had broken out aboard his schooner while he and the countess were drunk. He and his friends had gone on a vacation trip to hunt in the jungles and in the Gulf of Guinea came across the Angel Girl shortly after midnight and saw that she was on fire. He and his friends had boarded her and rescued Edith and so forth, leaving out the gruesome details of the fight and the death of Sir Henry and his mistresses.

When Captain Beasley entered the boat, he stood up in the stern and shook hands with his friends, warning them to keep a good lookout for native proas filled with blacks who would board the Jenny and kill every lubber aboard of her.

Waving to the men on deck who stood at the rail peering down at him, he told the bosun to push off. Black Jack muttered, "That is the last we shall see of our Yankee friend, Victor."

"You know you don't believe that, Jack," laughed Victor.

"Sure! Jud is daft, but I'm a blasted liar!" Jack said, as the three friends went aft upon the poop deck where they stood gazing through their binoculars.

A half hour later, Barkley said grimly, "The boat has landed. I wonder what will happen next?"

29
FACE TO FACE WITH CAPTAIN MORT

The cliff upon which the castle was built faced south and reached down to the water's edge, one hundred and twenty feet below. The rear of the castle butted up against the cliff that towered above. A white graveled path led from the castle gate to the stockades and the overseer's houses, a fifth of a mile distant.

On the hill above the stockades, stood the overseers houses; long, squat looking buildings that were furnished comfortably, but not luxuriously, as was the residence of Captain Mort, whom Jud Beasley knew to be the father of Sir Henry Mortimer Draker, who had gone to the bottom of the gulf in a raging furnace.

From the beach where the boat had landed was a rugged, winding trail that led up to the castle gate, between huge boulders. In places, it was so narrow that one had to squeeze through; only four foot wide. Fifty feet from the gate, the path broke out into a clearing and led along the cliff and around a bend in the path that was but three feet from its edge. One false step and a man would topple over it into the gulf below.

After conversing with his men, Jud told the bosun to keep a good lookout for native proas, to watch for his return with Captain Mort. If alone, he should clap the irons on him and take him aboard. He then left them with a handshake and a smile upon his face. The moment he passed from view, the bosun chuckled, "Jimmy, you and me will trail our Yankee skipper and see what kind of a reception he will meet with up at the castle. Hand us a couple of them cutlasses, mates. Keep a damned good lookout, the rest of you lubbers; if you hear me whistle, me hearties, come a running and bring them other pig-stickers along with you."

"Aye, aye, sir!" they replied, as the bosun and Jimmy trailed along the path behind Captain Beasley.

The inaction, the waiting, irked the men aboard the schooner. It frazzled their nerves. They stood on the port and starboard side of the schooner watching the water's of the gulf. On the fo'c'sle deck were two of the men lying flat on their stomachs peering over the bows. Aft on the poop deck stood the three navigators gazing through their binoculars. Down below deck, the Belle of Grimsby was sleeping, dreaming of Captain Beasley and the lovely girls in the castle on the hill.

Black Jack had told the men after the boat had left the schooner that if Captain Beasley did not return with Captain Mort at the stipulated time, four bells, they should follow him and Victor ashore to the castle on the hill.

They told him they would. Not one man would lift a hand to man the ship until they knew what was what.

Barkley, the mate, had told Black Jack that he had something say about it. He had his orders from Captain Beasley, and so forth, to which the two friends laughed aloud.

"Jim, orders or no orders, we are going to butt into that castle if Judson Beasley don't turn up. Neither you, Victor, or I could do a damn thing about it. Them fishermen for'ard would just grin at us and clap you in irons if you tried to prevent them from going ashore."

"That would be mutiny," Barkley said, weakly.

"All right, Jim. Victor, the admiral of the Barstow fleet would give them lubbers orders to man the boat and follow him, along with this lubber. What could you do about it, me hearty?"

"Nothing!"

"Righto!" Black Jack had said, laughing.

Captain Beasley had approached the gates of the castle boldly and suddenly found himself confronted by two giant black men, whose long lances held him at a distance, the points of them pressed against his breast.

"Stop that, you scum!" he roared at them. "I am the mate of the Angel Girl that is anchored way off the Bight. Captain Henry sent me ashore with a message for his father, Captain Mort. See this ring?" he asked, holding it out before them. "If I have any more of your damned nonsense, I'll report you to Captain Mort. Open up the gate and be quick about it."

The two West Indian Negroes, who prided themselves on being Englishmen, grinned at Captain Beasley and lowered their lances. One of them staring seaward muttered, "Ay no see lights of schooner."

"How in hell can you? Do you suppose that we lay at anchor with all lights showing after having a run in with a gun boat? However, just cast your weather eyes there, a little westward. You can see her white sails fluttering in this off-shore breeze. I know you English Negroes have the best sight of any men I ever met in life. Come on, open up that gate or you'll wish you were back in the West Indies."

Unheeding the command, the Negroes stood gazing out at sea. One of them, rubbing his eyes, said he saw the schooner and his mate muttered, "I see her now, too."

Captain Beasley had them seeing things. He muttered inwardly, "The damned liars!" as the Negroes conversed together for a few moments at the gate, glancing at Captain Beasley and the ring he was twirling around his finger with grim satisfaction.

With the butt of their spears, they banged on the gate, once, a pause, twice, a pause, then thrice, more loudly. With crunch and groan, the heavy oaken gates made from some of the timbers of the old Spitfire swung inward.

"Captain Mort in der," one of the guards said, pointing to another massive gate that led to an inner court.

Jud nodded, but he seemed to be in no hurry now; he stood for a few moments after glimpsing the two stalwart Negroes who guarded the gate in the courtyard, sizing up the place. He noted that the outer courtyard wherein he stood was semi-circular and cut out of the rocky formation of the cliff upon which the castle was built.

He observed that there were stone steps leading up to the outer ramparts where three twelve pounders were mounted; guns that covered the Bight and stockades a thousand feet beyond; guns that were taken from the old wreck of the Spitfire.

Across the courtyard, almost in the center of it, stood a great stone dais from which rose a massive oaken cross. He stared at it amazed as the Negroes pointed to the gate. Jud had taken less than a minute making his observations.

He told himself that if he had to get away from the infernal den in a hurry, the only chance he would have for doing so, seeing that the outside gate had closed upon him cutting off his exit that way, would be to climb those steps to the ramparts and if he could not reach the cliffs above, to dive into the black waters of the gulf. He shuddered at the thought, then laughed.

"Come on, you big chunks of black ebony; what in hell are you waiting for? Where is Captain Mort?"

They pointed to the gate and muttered, "Captain Mort come soon. No disturb now."

Jud Beasley became impatient. He advanced toward the gate but the points of the lances in the hands of the two Negroes held him back. "My message is important. Captain Henry..."

The inner gates swung open heavily. He stood spell-bound for a moment or two gazing at the occupants of the elaborately furnished den. Then he stepped within and he saw a half dozen lovely girls in their rich, silken robes and diamond rings, bracelets and necklaces, reclining at the foot of a raised dais upon tigers and lions skins, their graceful arms resting upon their heads. Above them sat the monster in his Turkish robes of red, emblematic of the blood he had shed in his years of piracy and slavery on the Middle Passage. At last, he was face to face with Captain Mort.

As he advanced toward him, he noted a lovely dancing girl in the circle. His intrusion into the circle brought Captain Mort to his feet. He stood scowling a moment at Beasley, then thundered, "who in hell are you?"

Jud Beasley ignored the direct question and began to twirl around his finger the ring he had taken from the finger of a dead man. Then he laughed outright and said, "Do you recognize this ring, Captain Mort? You do, then you should know that I have a message for you from Captain Henry. He is dying and I urge you to get into a pair of pants as quickly as possible and return with me aboard the Angel Girl – if you wish to see him alive."

30
THE LOVELY CAPTIVE'S FATE

When the bosun and Jimmy Grimes saw Captain Beasley enter the castle and the gates close behind him, they lost no time in returning to the boat where their mates awaited them. They quickly told them of what had occurred and immediately the bosun told them to pull back to the schooner, Jenny.

"Blimey, Bill, if Captain Beasley don't return on time, we'll grab them blacks and make 'em open up them gates," Jimmy said.

"Maybe! I dunno but what it would be best to close their mouths and try to get into the castle by way of them bloomin' ramparts. We could get a hook on to the top, I'm thinking, and shinny up the ropes in a jiffy and surprise them lubbers inside, if necessary. Anyway, I daresay we got time to report to Black Jack and Victor that our captain got inside but could not get out without our help, if he be detained there."

While they were reporting those facts to the officers aboard the Jenny, Jud stood staring at the old devil before him. On either side of him stood two slaves of the Fellah tribe, waving over Captain Mort their long, palm fans. Around the courtyard stood a half dozen big Negroes, some ten paces apart, with their long lances at rest upon the timbered floor. Between them, in brackets on the walls, glowed torches that flashed upon their almost naked bodies, making them look like statues of polished, black ebony.

Nearer the dais stood three white men, whose richly embroidered robes could not hide the unmistakable evidences of their former occupation. Not one of them hid the marks of battle upon their ugly countenances. In their belts were long, jeweled dirks. They stood glaring at Jud with scowling faces and arms folded, as Captain Mort blazed, "To whom am I indebted for this intrusion? Answer me, you damned lubber and stop grinning."

Jud laughed. Evading the question for a few moments, he said, casually, "You've got a great outfit here, Captain Mort. I'll tell the world you have."

The lovely girls at his feet were smoking their perfumed cigarettes that sent up a subtle odor into his nostrils. Again, he glimpsed the lovely dancing girl in the circle, who stood with drooping head and furtive gaze, staring at the handsome intruder. Again Captain Mort thundered, "Are you deaf, you damned lubber? Who and what are you?"

Jud came to the conclusion that he had aroused the curiosity of the old devil and immediately replied, "I'm Judson Bennet, first mate of the Angel Girl with a message for you from Captain Henry. If you want to see him alive again, I urge you to get into a pair of pants and return with me. Say, what in the devil were you about to do to that lovely dancing girl yonder?" he asked, turning his gaze upon her to find a pair of pleading eyes meeting his own.

Evading Jud's question, Captain Mort stepped down from the dais that was covered with a dozen or more Persian and Turkish rugs.

"Give me the token," he demanded, holding out his left hand.

Jud had been waiting for that request. He twirled it around his finger. A moment later, he handed it to Captain Mort. The latter turned it over in his hand and smiled. So did Captain Beasley.

"The token! It is from my son. What cargo have you brought for me?"

"Brandy, champagne, wines, and fruit from the Port of Funchal."

"What has detained you? You are ten days late," Captain Mort grouched.

"Captain Henry can give you that information; he can tell you of the bloody fight we had. One of her Majesty's gun boats chased us. We had to show her a clean pair of heels and head out to sea just as we were entering the gulf."

"No British gun boat would interfere with the "Angel Girl," commanded by my son," growled Captain Mort.

"All right, Captain. I'm a damned liar! You can prove my assertions true or false. If I have lied to you, you can hang me from the peak of the mizzen sail," Jud blurted.

"What became of Sandy McIntosh—the first mate of the Angel Girl?"

"I guess you know what happened to him and Bloody Pedro likewise," Jud told him, grinning, as he turned a thumb upside down, which brought a smile to the face of Captain Mort.

"All right. I'll be with you shortly." Clapping his hands, he roared, "Proceed with the festivities."

Jud was amazed. He sense the fact that the old devil was still suspicious. "Cut it short, Captain. Captain Henry is dying. He has a sea chest in the lazarette he wants you to bring ashore. I offered to bring it along with he, but he objected, telling me he wanted to see his father once more, before he…"

"Oh yes. The sea chest. Where did you come from?"

"I was in charge of the blacks at Walfish Bay that Captain Manley of the Mary Jane landed there. I transported them across country to the mines. We must get to going, Captain. If I had time, I'd be tickled to death to stay here and spend a night," he told the slaver with a sly wink.

Captain Mort smiled, then nodded, as his three old white retainers stood before him, throwing him a sly wink as much as to say, 'That lubber is lying, Captain. We await your pleasure.'

That is what Jud thought. He had watched their actions closely. He stood smiling with his hand on the hilt of his sword, ready to cut down the three ruffians if they attacked him. He saw Captain Mort wink back with his left eye and the next moment his retainers bowed and stepped back to one side, scowling at Captain Beasley.

Several of the slave girls, almost nude, like the giant Negroes who stood around the circle who were maids of the white captive girls of the harem, passed around the reclining figures with gold and silver goblets of wine. After the last girl had been served, they raised their glasses on high and from their lips came the cry, "To our lord and master! Confusion to his enemies and death to those who rebel against his will!"

Jud could not refrain from saying, "Some toast that, but I could give a better."

Later, he understood the meaning of that toast. Captain Mort snarled at him, clapped his hands again, and some of the black slaves led the dancing girl to the outer court. There, a heavily upholstered chair of antique design was carried out and placed for the monster. He sat down facing the cross, as some of the slave girls led the trembling white, dancing girl to the raised dais where a giant Negro, who had followed, placed her against the cross. In a few moments, her arms were bound to it and one of the slave girls tore the robe from her bosom, exposing her lovely pink and white breasts. With one pleading glance at Captain Beasley, her head fell forward as one of the Zanaboris tribe of Negroes mounted the three steps with an evil grin upon his face; in his hand a whip made of a dozen rawhide thongs.

"Good God!" breathed Jud, inwardly. "Surely that devil is bluffing."

"Your fate, my beauty, rests entirely in your hands. Submit yourself, soul and body to my will and live in a dream of splendor, or meet death upon the cross at the hands of that man," the black devil of hell told her.

A shudder passed through the delicate frame of the young woman, who was in her middle twenties, Jud thought. Casting an appealing glance at Jud, she swooned and hung limp upon the cross.

Jud was about to bound up the steps when the girl lifted her head and murmured, "I tell you, you black-hearted devil, that I will never submit to your will. God forbid!"

Jud stood rooted to the spot, thinking. He knew that if he intervened in her behalf, he alone could not save the girl; that he likewise would meet death at the hands of the retainers surrounding Captain Mort. While he was thinking thus, Captain Mort, with blazing eyes, clapped his hands again.

The big Negro raised his whip and, as he was about to bring it down across the breast of the girl, Jud sprang up the steps, wrenched it from his hand and brought the heavy butt of it down on the head of the Negro. The brute shook his head for a moment only. As he was about to grapple with Jud, the Yankee drew his sword and cut him down. He rolled down the steps to the feet of Captain Mort, dead. Jud had decided. His doom was sealed by that act.

31
A PRISONER IN THE DUNGEONS

Captain Beasley was occupied with defending himself from the dagger thrusts of the three white retainers of Captain Mort, who looked on gloatingly. As Jud struck two of the ruffians down to rise no more, he was wondering why the statue-like forms with lances at rest did not rush at him.

The third ruffian, wounded in the shoulder, with blood dripping down his silken, embroidered shirt, had backed away with a howl of rage upon his lips as Jud turned to face the Negroes.

"Come on, you! Let me mingle the blood of these white hellions with yours. Come on, blast you!" he roared, then turned to face Captain Mort upon whose face was a grin of admiration.

"This is no laughing matter, Captain. It was their life or mine," he cried as he sprang up the steps and in the twinkling of an eye cut the thongs that bound the girl to the cross.

Encircling the girl with his left arm, in his right the sword, he came down from the dais and faced Captain Mort.

"By the right of conquest, Captain Mort, that I am sure you uphold, this girl is mine. Come on! Let's get to going. Captain Henry, ever fair and just, will marry us when out at sea, if he lives. If, however, he is dead by now, you have only yourself to blame."

"Where did you get that sword" He held his white hand out for it, but Jud ignored the action. "I seem to recall having seen it in the hands of the man I hung from the yardarm of my old ship, the Spitfire."

"Perhaps, I don't know, but Captain Henry presented it to me for saving his life," he lied.

"Captain Henry took it from the man I hanged—a man you resemble. I wonder if…"

He paused, clapped his hands thrice and in a moment the black statues came to life. They surrounded Jud and the girl. The points of their lances were pressed against him, waiting for the signal to kill him.

"Wait, you blasted lubbers! This brave adventurer I reserve for a better fate. But, upon my return from the Angel Girl, if I find you've lied to me, you'll end your days in chains in the dungeons below with that rebellious wench!" roared Captain Mort, as he stepped down and took the sword from Beasley.

For one fleeting moment, Jud thought to run it through the old devil, but he realized how futile it would be. A half dozen lances would pierce him through the next moment, and the girl, undoubtedly. While there was life in his body, there was hope, he told himself, and handed the sword over with a smile on his face.

The captive girls of the harem and their graceful maids were staring at the Yankee with wide open eyes. Upon the faces of the former, horror had given place to undisguised admiration, even while almost at their feet lay the bodies of the giant Negro and two white men, still in death.

Again clapping his hands, armed Negroes came pouring through doors on each side of the dais in the inner court.

"Take this man and girl below to the dungeons and see to it that they do not escape. Chain them together, but if one hair of their heads is injured during my absence, I'll have you thrown to the alligators in the swamps."

To others who stood with lances grounded, he roared, "Take that dead carrion out of my sight through the secret tunnel. The alligators in the swamps there can thank this son of a sea-wolf for a meal tonight." Turning to Jud with a smile that was half sneer, "Well, my brave and chivalrous friend, what have you to say now?"

"I repeat, that I be permitted to marry this girl. Take us both aboard the Angel Girl, Captain. Can't you see that my only reason for interfering in your plan was that I had fallen madly in love with this beautiful girl?" he said, earnestly, as the girl gazed up into his face amazed and delighted, as she clung to his arm.

"That sounds fair enough, my friend! But I must keep you both within bounds during my absence. If your story is true, you and the girl can go with my blessing. Away with the prisoners," he commanded.

"You win!" Jud conceded, calmly, "But for the love of God get to going. Say, Captain Mort, before you get into your pants and leave for the Angel Girl, I beg of you to rustle up some food for me. I'm just about starved."

Captain Mort was not without a sense of humor. He eyed Jud, smiling, for a few moments and, notwithstanding he had raised hell in that courtyard and killed three of his men, he could not refrain from admiring the man who had so calmly faced him and his retainers that night.

"You're a brave man, Bennet, and I might—well, even if you have lied to me, you shall, if you wish, serve me here in my castle as my honored friend and first officer. Furthermore, the girl shall be yours. I swear it!"

"I'll take you up on that," Jud said, knowing that such suggestions were vain indeed. "I'll be waiting for your return, but don't forget that food you promised me," he said, as Captain Mort turned his thumb upside down.

32
ALONE WITH THE DEAD

The flickering lights in the brackets on the walls cast around that horrible dungeon—a dungeon cut out of the rocky cliffs and braced with heavy timbers—revealed to Jud's horrified gaze three men chained and shackled to the timbers. Two of them were lying down, asleep, he thought. Each and every one of them living skeletons, shadows of their former selves.

One, who sat on his haunches against one of the timbers, glared at him and the girl with madness in his eyes—eyes sunken deep in their sockets.

When Jud and the girl were chained and shackled to a timber facing him and they were left alone with the exception of one of the guard's who stood with his long lance at rest a dozen paces away, he asked, "Who are you, my friend? Why are you here? What have you done to merit such fiendish treatment as this?"

"I was once, ages ago, it seems, the overseer at the stockades. I objected to Captain Henry's deviltry one night he came ashore. He took my mistress, a lovely Egyptian girl, away from me, and sent her aboard the three-masted schooner, Sea Witch. He had me take a message to Captain Mort and from that day I have been a prisoner here in this dungeon. Lallah, Lallah, Lallah!" he moaned, as his starved body rocked from side to side.

"And these men?" Jud asked, pointing to his two companions who had never moved.

"They are men who sailed with Captain Henry. Two of his second mates, they told me, who had rebelled against Captain Henry's will and objected to his deviltry aboard the schooner, bringing lovely girls to Captain Mort's harem. They are, like myself, doomed to die in chains. And God help you and that lovely creature by your side, as you see us, even so will you two be eventually," he moaned, commiseration showing in his skeleton-like countenance for the newly arrived prisoners.

"Well, that damned old slaver has got me in a tight place, my friend, but I don't aim to stay in it long. Here comes the tommy, as the Sons of the Sea call it," he laughed.

"Not for me," moaned the miserable, dying wretch, glaring madly at the two Negroes who were then placing a feast before the astonished eyes of the Yankee.

"You can bet your sweet life you are going to join in this reception I'm giving before that bloody murderer returns," Jud said, after the departure of the slaves.

Turning to the girl by his side, he asked, "Who are you, girlie? Your voice brings pleasant and painful memories to me. I am a bean-eater from Boston, Massachusetts. What part of the States are you from; the east, I'll swear," he told her as he began to carve up a roast suckling pig and serve it to her with all the accessories, while the starved overseer sat gazing upon the feast that was just beyond his reach, licking his parched lips with a tongue that darted out of his cavernous mouth like the fangs of a rattlesnake.

The girl smiled sadly up at Jud and informed him that she was Marion De Kalb, a banker's daughter, from Brooklyn, New York. While she and her parents were sojourning in Paris, she had made the acquaintance of the Countess Catherine Du Bois. Later, she was introduced to Sir Henry Mortimer Draker and consented, without informing her parents, to take a trip with them across the channel to London.

She said she thought it would be great fun, that the hue and cry after her would surely be...."

She broke down and began sobbing, bitterly, as Jud handed her a silver plate with a goodly portion of roast pig.

"Go on," he suggested, gently, as he went on carving.

"I was a most foolish and vain-glorious girl. I thought my picture would be in all the papers, but instead of going to London, the schooner headed down the coast here."

She said that one night Sir Henry had given the countess a sleeping powder and he had entered her room and...."

She broken down again, then, still sobbing, she concluded, "I refused to become his mistress. Upon our arrival here, I was placed in Captain Mort's harem and have spent my time dancing, always dancing, amusing that old devil, Captain Mort."

Jud could hardly believe that the countess would have betrayed one of her own sex into the hands of Captain Henry and yet, he knew for a fact that she took part in tricking the daughter of Lady Moresby in like manner.

"The countess was a most fitting companion for Sir Henry, but my dear, they are both dead!"

"Dead?"

"I'll tell the world they are. That devil poisoned the countess and her maid Lallah. But before Lallah died, she killed Captain Henry and his spy, the mulatto steward. She knifed them in the back," he said grimly, "and....."

"Lallah, Lallah, my Lallah!" moaned the grinning skeleton, who had been listening to Jud telling the girl of what had happened to her abductors and the schooner.

"Eat, girlie," he pleaded. "We may never get another feed like this again. Let us be merry for the moment, Marion, for when that old devil returns, you can bet your bottom dollar if he does so that hell will be popping. I lied to him. I wanted to get him aboard my schooner that is anchored in a cove and hang him to the masthead as he hung my father from his."

The growls of the famished man brought Jud back to his surrounds. The guard stood up at the farther end of the dungeon, near the stone steps leading to the court above. He cut off a goodly portion of the small pig for himself and cast over to the miserable creature the remains of it. Sufficient for two good, hearty men.

The overseer, like a famished wolf, began to tear the flesh to pieces and gulp it down ravenously.

Marion had scarcely touched a bite of the pig. "Eat," Jud counseled. "We must preserve our strength. God only knows what tomorrow may bring."

"And I the cause," she sobbed.

"No, no," he comforted her. "I took a chance when I entered this nest of evil, Marion; I did it with my eyes wide open. That crafty devil suspected me. He probably saw in me a great resemblance to the man he hung from the yardarm of his ship. That's about the size of it. I should have grown a beard. However, don't worry about me. If I had not interfered in your behalf, I should be lying here in chains just the same. I am a fatalist, Marion, and believe in my heart and soul that we shall both leave this dungeon alive. When we do, that poor lubber is going with us.

"But tell me, Marion," gazing into the uplifted blue-grey eyes of the girl, "have you been the mistress of that old slaver, Captain Mort?" he was gentle, but insistent.

Her eyes widened. "No! I scratched his face and he condemned me to dance before him, night after night, almost nude. After several months, he informed me that my time was short. Unless I yielded myself to him tonight, I would be whipped then sold into slavery to some king inland. I – I – am a virgin," she told him with hand covered eyes.

"Well, we ain't dead yet, Marion. Lots can happen," he tried to cheer her. "Someday, you will meet your parents face to face again, dear."

"I cannot visualize such happiness. We are lost!" she declared.

"Maybe not," Jud maintained, grimly.

The Negro on guard came and prodded the overseer with his lance, grinning like the devil.

"Stop that, blast you! Let the man sleep. He ain't got long to live, "I'm sure."

"He dead," the Negro grunted.

"Wake up those other men," Jud commanded.

The giant black stared at him. "They dead an hour ago."

"Good Lord, Marion! Here we are, alone with the dead."

"Their sufferings are ended. Ours scarcely begun," she sobbed.

"I wonder," mused Jud, "if my men did as I told them. If so, Marion, then Captain Mort is in chains aboard of my schooner. Cheer up," he laughed, "if he were not so, he would have returned by this time, I'm sure."

A terrific din, howls of rage and the clashing of steel came faintly to his ears from above. He laughed madly. The girl glanced up at him.

"Listen!" he suggested.

"What has happened?" she asked.

"Someone is raising hell up there in the courtyard, I guess," he told her as he sat straight upright, as much as his chains permitted and began to sing, loud and long, "Sons of the Sea".

33
THOU ART OF THE BLOOD-BROTHERHOOD

The moment Jud and the young woman were taken below to the
dungeon, Captain Mort gazed around upon the beautiful, richly
gowned women of his harem, most of whom had, before they entered
that den of evil, been mistresses of Sir Henry aboard the schooner
"Angel Girl," until he had tired of them. Two, who had repulsed Sir
Henry, on the trip from Naples to the Gulf of Guinea had been rushed
to the castle on the hill. Unlike Marion, they had eventually become
mistresses of Black Mort, who was in his middle sixties. They had
preferred life there with him to that of being sold into slavery inland or
death by slow starvation in the dungeon below—after being whipped by
the giant Negro.

The rich robes the girls wore and those of the slaver and his
retainers had been purchased from time to time by the late Captain
Henry at Naples, Constantinople, and Paris; likewise the furnishings of
the castle and its Persian and Turkish rugs.

After the interrupted revels that night, Captain Mort had sent the
girls to their luxuriously furnished rooms above, followed by their
graceful slave maids who waited attendance upon them in their
separate boudoirs. After placing their jewels aside, nonchalantly, they
bathed in sweet-scented water and donned silken pajamas and slippers
and then proceeded to a large room and began chattering away like so
many parrots in a gilded cage. French and Italian, with a spattering of
English were all one to the slave girls who sat at their mistresses feet
gazing up into the lovely faces.

They were talking about the Yankee who had dared to enter the domain of their lord and master of the castle; the man who had so bravely defended their rebellious companion in captivity.

It was but a moment after they had retired when Captain Mort glared at the last of his white retainers, Samuel Thorpe, who was at one time bosun of the Spitfire.

"I was thinking, Sam, that there might be some truth in the report of the sea wolf below. If not, how come he is in possession of my son's ring? The token that no man but he, myself, and my faithful guards know of that will admit a messenger to my presence."

"Isn't it possible, Captain, that the men aboard the Angel Girl mutinied and assisted the Yankee to overpower Captain Henry and clap him in irons or murder him. And, with the ring in his possession he had learned in some way or other, was the key that would open the gates for him. He came to entice you aboard the schooner and take you back to London in chains, where you are wanted so badly, as Captain Mort of the old piratical slaver Spitfire. You know," he grinned, "that the father of Sir Henry is supposed to be dead; you died of the sleeping sickness exploring the dark continent of Africa. As Captain Mort, you would get your neck stretched upon the scaffold," he concluded, with a broad grin upon his face that bore the marks of battle in the days gone by.

"No, by God! It is not possible, Sam, that the scum of the Middle Passage in the fo'c'sle would risk their necks by landing on the shores of England. That I am sure of; but there may be something in what you say. Perhaps the countess fell in love with that handsome young devil, Bennet, and revealed to him what was what in the castle on the hill here. And, while my son was drunk, relieved him of the ring. In that case, it is evident to me that the countess got tired of my son and fearful of being brought here, planned...."

He had paused again and stood in thinking attitude, stroking his van-dyke beard, reflectively.

"Once there at the landing, Captain Mort," said his crafty lieutenant, "you will be seized by that Yankee's men. I have not the slightest doubt but what he has told them he would take them all back to the States with him and set them ashore there. Anyway, I feel there is some deviltry afoot. I feel it in my bones," he said placing his hand on the wound of his left shoulder that Jud had inflicted upon him.

"Ha, ha, ah!" laughed the old slaver. "I doubt, Sam, if you have any bones—you blasted fat lubber! That wound was but a pin-prick. Follow me. Outside the courtyard we shall see the lights of the schooner Angel Girl off the Bight. You shall deliver a message to my son personally."

Sam Thorpe gulped. He had no liking for that job. He visualized himself a prisoner aboard the Angel Girl heading back to England and himself in prison there, waiting to have his fat neck stretched upon the scaffold. Craftily, he remarked, "Of course, Captain. Whatever you say. Orders is orders."

Captain Mort nodded. Then blazed, "God blast him!"

"Who? Sir Henry?" asked Sam.

"No, you blasted lubber! That damned Yankee below. If he has deceived me, I swear that you shall have the pleasure of slitting his throat from ear to ear and that the girl Marion will be yours. Now off with you to the schooner with a message to my son. I shall wait for you outside the outer gate," he told him, clapping his hands. The next moment the gate swung inward and, majestically, he strode out into the darkness with his hand upon the sword he had taken from Captain Beasley.

Sam followed. His face had paled. Cunningly, he said, "All right, Captain, I'm off to see Captain Henry."

He was about to depart on an errand that he never intended to fulfill, when Captain Mort bawled at him, "Wait, you lubber! I was doubtful of you, Sam. We will go together. Thou art of the blood-brotherhood, sworn to protect me."

The black retainers, who had stood at attention, followed the slaver and his lieutenant, who proceeded to the edge of the cliff.

"No lights showing, Sam. There is something wrong. You go ahead and try to discover what," he commanded, then roared, "Advance, guards! Advance, you black devils!"

A dozen pairs of eyes were gleaming at them through the pitchy blackness of the night and the voice of Black Jack Barstow rang out, "Up and at 'em, me hearties! Not one of the hellions must escape."

34
WHERE DID CAPTAIN MORT GO

A half hour after the bosun had reported to the officers aboard the
schooner Jenny that Captain Beasley had entered the castle and
that the massive gates had closed behind him, Black Jack, Victor, and
ten of the Grimsby fishermen landed on the white, sandy beach.

Silently, they picked their way up the rugged trail and surprised the
two Negro guards. Gagged and bound, they were dragged some fifty
feet or more away and tied together on the edge of the cliff, Jack telling
them that if they moved, they would roll over into the gulf below and
become food for the sharks. Those Negroes knew it. They lay perfectly
still. There was no use struggling. They realized that fact and fearfully
awaited their release, if ever.

Creeping back to the gate, Black Jack and five of his men on one
side, Victor and his on the other, they waited, it seemed an eternity, for
the gate to open up. Black Jack had just about decided that there was
nothing else to do but climb up to the ramparts above and surprise the
inmates when the gates swung inward. The fishermen waited for Black
Jack's command, as the slaver went to the edge of the cliff with Sam
Thorpe. Not seeing Jud with them, he sensed the fact that he was held
a prisoner in the castle. That decided his action.

Jud had heard the rumpus above and broke out into song, but his
men could not hear him. While the fishermen were engaged, cutting
and slashing at the Negroes, Black Jack singled out the old slaver and
Victor tackled his lieutenant, who had tried to return to the courtyard,
where the blacks themselves had retreated. One after the other
dropped to rise no more before the furious attack of the naval reserve

157

men who had been hand-picked by Black Jack Barstow from the fleet of Grimsby. Victor had the big, fat lubber, Sam Thorpe on his knees, pleading for mercy. He was wounded badly. He was disarmed and dragged aside to the foot of the steps leading to the ramparts above.

"One move out of you, you lubber," Victor told him, "and I'll finish you."

A dozen more Negroes poured into the outer courtyard, but there was no stopping the fishermen. They were laughing and yelling as they cut down those blacks. Some of the fishermen were slightly wounded, blood flowing down their arms, but they all stood on their feet while Victor yelled, "Give 'em hell, me hearties," as he cut the lance out of the hands of a giant Negro and with one sweep of his cutlass sent him crashing to the stone courtyard as other Negroes appeared on the scene.

For one moment only, Victor gazed back at Black Jack and Captain Mort in a fight to the death. Jack was yelling, "Surrender, you blasted old fool! For the past five years, I have longed to meet you and cut off that bloody head of yours. Throw down your sword, I tell you," he raged.

The strength in the old devil's arm surprised Black Jack, undoubtedly. He had all he could do to keep himself from being run through with the sword he knew had been taken from Captain Beasley. Black Jack's command brought a smile to the slaver's face as Jack tried to back him toward the edge of the cliff.

"After I have run you through and cut off your damned head, you whelp, I'll feed your carcass to the alligators in the swamps, blast you!"

"That's a bad guess," laughed Black Jack, as he brought his cutlass down with such force that, had it hit the old rascal, would have split him in two.

Before he recovered himself, Captain Mort lunged at him. The sword had pieced his left arm only. Except for a quick side movement on Black Jack's part, it would have cut through his heart. The next moment, Captain Mort dropped the sword with a howl of rage as his thumb was slashed off and in the twinkling of an eye, the slaver ran into the courtyard, turned and fired point blank at Black Jack. The shot grazed his temple. It stunned him for a moment as he staggered into the courtyard. The next moment Captain Mort had disappeared. Engaged as they were in mortal combat, none of the fishermen had noticed where the black devil went to. Victor's desire was to prevent any of the blacks escaping to inform the overseers at the stockades of what was going on. He and his men had done that and Black Jack commanded some of the men to close the gates. He was still dazed and stood gazing upon the shambles around him. The fight was now practically over, but the danger unabated. He believed that someone down at the stockades must have heard the terrific din up at the castle.

"By God, Victor, I had no chance to give you lubbers a hand. That Black Devil of hell, more than twice my age, put up a hell of a fight with Jud's sword. I'm damned lucky to be alive at this moment," he grinned.

"I daresay, Jack. But say, I wonder…"

Victor cut himself short, as one of the blacks, a guard from the dungeon, came into the courtyard and fell upon his knees. He was wounded only slightly. The bosun had got from him the information that Captain Beasley and a girl were in chains below. He and Jimmy Grimes had gone down there to release the captives, taking the key from the Negro.

"Avast there, Pat!" yelled Black Jack, as one of the fishermen were about to decapitate Captain Mort's lieutenant who was on his knees pleading for mercy. "We shall need that blighter. Where did Captain Mort go?" he questioned Sam Thorpe.

Victor was binding up his wounds. They had come prepared to give first aid to the wounded. Sam Thorpe, believing his life would be spared, replied immediately, "He went through one of the secret tunnels that leads to the stockades. He'll be up here in fifteen minutes with a hundred blacks at the back of him and drive every one of you into the swamps to become food for the alligators. Thanks!" he said to Victor and fell back against the stone walls of the courtyard as a voice yelled, "That's nice! Captain Mort has all the alligators tamed so that they won't make a meal out of him, eh! I think you are a damned liar, Sambo."

"What next, Captain Beasley?" asked Black Jack, while Victor stood staring at the girl who leaned upon Jud's arm with eyes closed. The horror of it all—the dead around them—had not escaped her, but bravely, she clung to her protector, as Jud barked, "Jimmy Grimes and Bill Davis up on the ramparts and man the guns. The guard in the dungeon said they were always ready for action and that there's plenty of ammunition up there. It is as dark as blazes, but you can see them blacks crawling up here on the white, sandy path leading from the stockades. Give them hell, me hearties, and hold them back. I've got lots of work to do here, yet."

While this was going on, Victor had given first aid to Black Jack and the rest of the men whose wounds were light. He turned to gaze at Jud and found the girl's eyes upon him. He smiled encouragingly at her, as Jud told some of his men to drag the dead into the dungeons below, for what he contemplated doing next was to locate the girl captives and take them out of the infernal den forever. He visualized those delicate creatures entering such a shambles, even while he wondered why Marion had not swooned away the moment she entered it. Then he caught her smiling at Victor and the latter's eyes upon Marion. Even at that dreadful moment, he told himself that, if they lived to get back to Grimsby, there would be one less bachelor in the Grimsby fleet.

"What became of the two outer guards, Jack?"

"By jove, Jud, I quite forgot them lubbers," Jack confessed. "If they have not rolled off the cliff into the gulf below they are outside yet. We grabbed them and trussed them up like a couple of lunatics."

"Get them inside quickly, then close and bar the gates, Victor."

"Aye, aye, sir!" said Victor grimly, wondering if it were possible that some of the men from the stockade had gone along the cliffs and were ready to swoop down on them from above.

With a couple of his men, Tom Lawler and Pat McShane, both young fellows in their middle twenties, they swung the heavy gates open, inch by inch, peering out in the darkness beyond with cutlasses in hand. Black Jack barked at them as the gate was closing, "Victor, ring four bells when you get back with them lubbers." Victor grinned and cautiously, after gazing around, approached the guards.

"Here we are me hearties," he said to the Negroes as he cut them adrift and the three of them lifted to their feet. "Captain Mort wants you fellows along with him in the tunnel leading to the swamps."

The Negroes were silent for obvious reasons. A stone in a twisted handkerchief filled their mouths. Not until they were safely in the courtyard did Victor remove them. There, he found the stewards and cooks of the castle who had been rounded up by the bosun and two of the fishermen. Captain Beasley commanded, "Drive every lubber into that secret tunnel leading to the swamps and bar and lock those doors. You," he grinned, at the last white retainer of Captain Mort, "will make a damn good feed for one of the alligators, I'm sure."

"For God's sake, Captain, don't send me through that tunnel," he pleaded, as he stood up, groggily on his feet. "Give me a chance. No man passing through those swamps could live."

"I get you! Being a white retainer, I'll give you that chance. Take my pistol and blow out your brains. What say?"

"I'll go through the tunnel," he growled, as the fishermen herded the Negroes to the door in the inner courtyard that led to the swamps. In five minutes they were behind the heavy oaken door that was locked, bolted, and barred likewise.

There were two tunnels the West Indian Negroes had told Captain Beasley about. He said that one branched off to the swamps and the other to the stockades. Sam Thorpe knew it and when driven into the tunnel, he, who was apparently near the end of the trail, suddenly came to life. He and the Negroes who were uninjured made their way along the tunnel toward the stockades, where Captain Mort had preceded them. The going was slow due to the fact they had to feel their way in the impenetrable darkness to prevent them from dashing their brains out against the jagged rocks. Furthermore, fifty feet from its exit was a door that had been closed behind Captain Mort, locked, bolted and barred. They were trapped.

Captain Mort had lost no time in rousing the overseers and over a hundred Negroes. The fishermen knew not of the danger that portended until suddenly they were startled by the booming of the guns on the ramparts above.

Stanley McShane

35
STAND BY THE GUNS

❝I was hoping," said Captain Beasley, "that we would be able to get down to the boats before those at the Bight discovered what was going on up here. It is my belief that Captain Mort managed to reach the stockades. In that case, we may yet have a fight before us. Our progress will be impeded greatly by the ladies. I don't aim to leave them lovely girls here in this hell hole."

Black Jack and Victor nodded. The former said, "I agree with you, Jud. That would be unthinkable. But for God's sake, get busy and let us get out of this as quickly as possible."

"A couple more of you men give a hand up there on the ramparts. Keep that scum off the sands. Take Victor's binocular along with you, Pat. It will be more useful up there, I'm sure," said Captain Beasley, as he glanced, distastefully, around the courtyard.

"Some of you men get into the kitchen. You will find sufficient water in the tanks there to wash down decks before..."

He turned away, smiling sadly, then beckoned to Marion and asked her to lead the way up to the boudoirs above and inform the girls that he was taking them back to civilization with him aboard of his ship.

The girls were delighted. They packed their filmly, silken garments into a chest while Jud was investigating the quarters of Captain Mort. He stood before a chest laughing.

"I don't know what is in there, men, but I'm mighty damned curious about it. Anyway, I need another sea chest aboard ship. Lug that out of here down by the gate and come back immediately."

162

It was a heavy chest, but the brawny fishermen handled it quite easily. When they deposited it by the gate where Black Jack and Victor stood in listening attitude, the former asked, "What in hell is that, Tom?"

"Captain Beasley's sea chest, sir!" the fisherman told him, as they went back upstairs grinning.

"Well, I'll be damned!" exploded Black Jack.

From the ramparts above, the guns were still booming. Below in the courtyard, men were busy slushing down. When they got through, each man began to sharpen his cutlass upon the floor. Some of them were grinning, telling Barstow and Victor that some of the nuts they had cracked had dulled them greatly, as Jud appeared upon the scene with a bevy of lovely girls. Victor stared at them amazed; then he caught Marion's gaze upon him. She was smiling at him. She saw nothing but those soft, brown eyes of his at that moment.

The lovely costumes the girls wore were more fitted for an occasion of life, love, and laughter in the ballrooms of Paris then in that den of evil. Behind them thronged the graceful slave girls.

Jimmy Grimes ran down from the ramparts, looking like a white-washed black. He stood petrified for a moment gazing at the lovely creatures before him. He gulped, then spouted, "Captain Beasley, we blasted every black from the path leading up to the castle, but I have an idea that them buggers are climbing the cliffs and will be dropping down upon the ramparts. Lots of powder left, but no shot, sir!"

"Call all hands below. To the boats! Keep your eyes peeled and cutlasses ready. No man knows what we shall find outside that gate and on the trail down to the boats."

Black Jack and Victor opened the gates, cautiously. They peered out into the darkness beyond. They stepped outside and glanced up at the cliffs above, through their binoculars. There was no danger from that direction. They were confident that they could reach the boats in safety.

Four men, lugging the two chests, followed behind the bosun, Bill Blake and Jimmy Grimes. The girls and their slave maids picked their way gingerly over the rugged trail. The going was slow. The three friends brought up the rear. A moment later Jud ran back to the castle. Black Jack turned and wondered what had happened to him. He grouched, "Go ahead, Vic. That blasted Yankee is daft. What in hell is the matter with the man?"

Before Victor could answer, he ran back toward the gates, but before he arrived there, Jud came out and with a grim smile on his face met Jack and told him, "I had a little job to finish back there in the castle, Jack. I was reminded of it at the last moment. We have got to get along more quickly. Every man who is able must carry one of those girls to the boats."

Victor had heard his making that suggestion. He lost no time in telling Marion who repeated the order to the girls. The next moment he had Marion in his arms, hers around his neck.

The girls understood. They had no objection to being carried in the arms of those brave fishermen. In fact, they were delighted. Their feet, covered only with sandals, had become exceedingly sore. The slave girls trailing behind them did not seem to mind that journey down to the boats. They were all bare-footed and went down that rough trail like so many mountain goats, their every movement one of grace.

They had almost reached the boats when a terrific blast rent the air from the castle on the hill. Flames rose high up above the cliffs.

"What was that, Jud?" asked Black Jack.

"The guns on the ramparts have gone into the gulf below. I wanted to make sure they would never be used again," he said, as the trail led down to the boats.

Jud's suggestion expedited their return and subsequently they reached the boats without mishap.

The slave girls evidently thought they were going along with their mistresses, but the boats were crowded. Jud said, sadly, I'm damn sorry we have to leave those poor girls behind us, but there's nothing we can do about it, mates. What in the devil could we do with them? We could not land them at Le Havre or in Grimsby. We would be up against a mighty bad proposition, surely."

"You are right about that, Jud. Look at the poor things!"

They had fallen upon their knees in the sands and with outstretched arms were chanting some dismal dirge that sounded like curses in the fishermen's ears. They were pleading to be taken along with their mistresses that they loved. The men turned their faces away. It was a most pitiful sight.

Barkley, the mate, had seen them getting into the boats, in the gray dawn of the morning that rose over the distant mountains. He was elated. He ran for'ard and weighed anchor. By the time the boats came alongside, it was up at the hawse pipe and as the men clambered aboard the head sails went up, hand over hand. He heard Jud yelling, who was the last man to leave the boats, "Be careful of those chests, men. Take them aft to the cabin."

Aboard the Jenny, the boats were taken inboard, just as the schooner headed out into the gulf with the ebb tide. Not until they passed out of the cove and were in sight of the stockades did the sails belly out with the light off-shore breeze.

When Jud went below, he found the women of the harem of Captain Mort peeking into every room. Marion opened Edith's door and the girls were met by the lovely, inquiring gaze of the girl who sat up in her berth. Marion went in and sat beside her, smiling, telling her that Captain Beasley and his men had rescued them from the harem. She and Jud had been confined in chains in the dungeon of the castle. Confidently, she told her that Jud had offered to marry her, but Captain Mort would not listen to such a proposal. She was about to tell her what had happened beforehand when Edith frowned and asked to be left alone, stating that she was very tired and not had a wink of sleep all night.

When Marion closed the door behind her, Edith fell to sobbing. She was jealous of the lovely girl, undoubtedly.

In the cabin, she found Captain Beasley attending the wounded men. Later, he left them and ran up on deck for Black Jack had communicated the fact to him that there were two native proas filled with blacks heading out from the Bight of the Niger.

"I see," he said, grimly. "Stand by to jibe over the foresail and head sheets, Jim. Victor and Black Jack can attend to the main. I'll run close in. she will turn in her own length. When on the starboard tack, have the men open up the ports and stand by the guns."

"Aye, aye, sir!" the mate replied, going for'ard.

36
CAPTAIN MORT LOSES HIS HEAD

Captain Beasley stood with his binoculars trained on the proas as they headed for the Jenny.

"In that foremost proa, I recognize Captain Mort. There's not enough wind right now for us to get safely away and prevent them blacks from boarding us on either side of the ship. They would swarm upon us and, while we could cut a lot of them lubbers down, they would eventually get the lot of us and take all the girls ashore there. So, it is up to us, Jack, to blast the lubbers out of the water."

"Righto, Jud, but we have little time to do it. They will be alongside in fifteen minutes.

The mate came aft. Jud told him, "Take the wheel, Jim. We will give them a surprise. Mort thinks that we are some coasting schooner. You, Victor, go below and calm the ladies. Tell them that I am destroying that castle on the hill. Do not permit one of them to come up on deck. Keep them all below—especially the Belle of Grimsby.

"Jim, bring her broadside when I tell you to luff." He ran for'ard, followed by Black Jack Barstow, saying, recklessly, "Sink the proas, Jud, and I'll dive overboard and bring that old devil back with me."

"The sharks would get you, Jack. Nothing would please me better than to have him aboard here and hang him, but that is out of the question. As long as he lives my work is not done. I had hoped that the alligators in the swamps had got the lubber as the guard said a door in the tunnel leading to the stockades was locked. He evidently had some means of opening it. I don't see that fat slob Sam Thorpe in the proas, but I do recognize the two overseers that I met up with, when I went ashore.

"Bosun, I want the bewhiskered devil's head off his shoulders. See him standing up in the stern of the foremost proa with his binoculars trained on us? He seems a bit suspicious. Open the gun ports, men. Let him see what is waiting for him—the welcome he is going to get," he laughed.

"Jimmy can hit the bugger in the bloomin' eye, Captain. Bill Davis and I can sink the proas. Say when," the bosun chuckled, spitting on his hands.

The two proas were about a cable's length away when Jud yelled, "Luff, Jim!" the next moment, when broadside, he told the gunners to fire.

A second later the two proas were scuttled, the shots killing some of the Negroes. The rest were floundering away, struggling to reach the beach, while the sharks that seemed to appear from nowhere, reduced their numbers to such an extent that little more than a score of the blacks succeeded in struggling out of the water.

"By the Lord, Jimmy, that shot of yours took off that lubbers head. Jibe the mainsail, men!"

While some of the fishermen were carrying out that order, Jud turned to the gunners, saying, "See them two houses on the hill there above the stockades? They are overseers. Get them, Jimmy! Bosun, you and Bill Davis destroy the stockades. Slaving on the Bight of the Niger will be finished for awhile and if it springs up again, it will not be commanded by Captain Mort and his hellions. That lubber, Mort, is now walking along the bottom of the gulf carrying his head in his arms, maybe in search of his son Sir Henry to hand him back his ring, the token. Ha, ha, ha! He exalted.

As the schooner glided out to sea, the guns boomed, again and again. Looking ashore, as the sun rose over the purple hills, they saw the overseers' houses on the hill crumble in ruins. The stockades were wrecked and burning. No life met their gaze upon the shore. What few had escaped had gone far beyond into the jungles.

"Jimmy, you're a wonder! The bosun and Bill are A-number-One gunners, but you are marvelous! Jud rejoiced.

"Tain't nothing, Captain. I hit the bloomin' flying jib-boom of the Angel Girl a half mile away. I could just as well brought down his foremast, but Captain Barstow objected. I couldn't miss that lubber's head—only a hundred feet distant," Grimes boasted, grimly.

The houses ashore were going up in smoke. Flames bellied high above the castle on the hill. The firing had ceased. There was practically nothing more to fire at. Nothing but death and desolation and flames raging inland. The edge of the forest that reached to the stockades had caught fire. A pall of black smoke rose above the ruins.

Captain Beasley and his friend Black Jack went aft. The latter remarked, "That was a good job well done, Jud. A job that should have been done by one of Her Majesty's gunboats long ago, but, of course," he laughed, "you know as well as I do that the lubbers who have made fortunes out of this business are men in the upper brackets, like the late Sir Henry. When he does not turn up in London, they will come to the conclusion that the Angel Girl foundered and went to the bottom with all hands, I daresay."

"You said it, Jack. I am wondering how Lady Moresby will take it— the loss of her dearly beloved friend?" Jud said, chuckling, as they climbed up to the poop. There, they found Victor peering ashore and neglecting his duty, for behind him had come a bevy of beauties on deck the next moment. There they stood gazing shoreward at the stockades and the castle on the hill, when suddenly, a terrific report reached them, and as they gazed at the still burning castle, smoke and ashes rolled high into the heavens, while burning timbers came down sizzling in the gulf.

"There goes your former residence, ladies," Jud told them with smiling eyes as they crowded round the friends and then, before they realized what was what, their lovely arms went round their necks and Jud roared, "Lay off that! Go below! Breakfast is served!"

"Imagine that!" laughed Black Jack. "Look at Victor!"

The latter was laughing. Jud believed Marion had put the girls up to expressing their appreciation to the officers for their delivery and destruction of the castle on the hill for the moment the girls had given that demonstration of their feelings, her arms had gone around Victor's neck and gently kissed him on the lips, again and again. Edith had remained below deck. When he went down, he met her face to face, but there was no welcoming smile upon it. She turned from him frowning.

"You ladies," he said, coolly, "will breakfast together at the first table. My friends and I can wait."

He ran up on deck again with a deep frown on his face. A moment later he said, "There was, undoubtedly, more shot and ammunition stored away in that castle. Some secret magazine I overlooked. Anyway, I took no chances of having them lubbers use the infernal den again. I fired the damn place before I left it, but I do wish it had been possible to take away all those Persian and Turkish rugs, the gold and silver plate, and hell knows what. Don't misunderstand me, my friends, I'm not inclined to be hoggish, but it did seem a damn shame to leave all that wealth behind us—to destruction. But..."

Black Jack interrupted, "Haven't you forgotten something? Something still left undone?" he winked at Victor and the mate.

"Righto! I was forgetting, me hearties," Jud agreed. "Captain Mort distracted my attention from it. After breakfast we will look into it," he grinned.

"Into what?"

"My sea chest, you lubber!' he laughed.

It was quite warm in the gulf as the schooner headed out to sea. On the return trip to Grimsby after the ladies had breakfasted, they came up on deck with smiling eyes and laughter upon their lips. Edith followed them and she stood on deck with Marion's arms around her waist gazing at the ruins of the castle on the hill, while Marion was conversing with her in whispers and the other girls chattering away in French and Italian.

Pat came aft to take the first trick at the wheel and relieved the mate. The four officers went below and sat at the second table, talking over the past events. When they rose from the table, Jud called the ladies below.

"Marion, will you kindly ask the girls what they intend doing after I land them at Le Havre, please. I do not speak French or Italian. I believe you do, Edith," he smiled, but she only nodded, became seated, and a moment later Marion sat by her side, telling Captain Beasley that the girls said it was their intention to go home. The jewels they had in their possession could be sold in Paris for sufficient to enable them to do so.

"Well, if I do not miss my guess, ladies, I have here in my sea chest a nice little nest egg that will..."

He broke off short, then threw up the lid of the chest and watching the faces of his friends and the girls who stood gasping with wide, staring eyes at the contents, he went on again, "There is a large fortune in this chest. The contents will make every one of you girls rich beyond avarice. Upon our arrival at Le Havre, the daughter of Lady Moresby and Marion will go ashore there on a shopping trip for you. You certainly cannot leave my schooner in those rich, silken robes you are wearing, there's no question about that. It should be quite obvious to one and all," he concluded. The next moment he and his friends went up on deck, leaving Edith and Marion to talk the matter over with the girls.

Black Jack and Victor had noticed the coldness of Edith's demeanor toward Captain Beasley. They figured she should be mighty proud of him. Here she was, safe aboard the schooner, homeward bound to England instead of being with Sir Henry in his villa at Naples, practically a prisoner there. They could not understand the Belle of Grimsby on that day. Black Jack told Victor that there would not be any wedding bells ringing out for Jud Beasley, the finest man they had ever met in life, but that he was damn sure they would ring long and loud for a lubber named Victor Jenson, admiral of the Barstow fleet.

"I daresay, Jack, there will be a double wedding and that my sister Jenny won't be breaking her heart any longer over a lubber like you," he retorted.

"By God, Victor!" laughed Jack, "since when did you become a mind-reader?"

Victor chuckled, but refrained from answering as Jud came and stood alongside of them, grimly silent. Victor had left his pipe below, intentionally or otherwise, and went down into the cabin and saw Edith and Marion seated together in silent converse. He smiled at Marion and said, "You are going to Grimsby with us, Marion, of course," while noting the fact that Edith's eyes were moist with suppressed tears.

"I am glad indeed, Victor, that I shall not be cast adrift at Le Havre, for I know that my parents have long since given me up for dead and returned home to Brooklyn, New York."

"Maybe I'll be seeing you home," he told her, as he snatched up his pipe and ran up on deck with glowing eyes, leaving smiles on the faces of both girls and Edith in a more contented frame of mind, for she read in their eyes the love of their souls for each other. Nevertheless, she continued to be cool to Judson Beasley because of his accusations, telling her that her silence had sent him in quest of the devil. Due to her extreme stubbornness and pride, she had not even asked Jack

Barstow if he had delivered the letter she had written to Jud at Oak Lodge and entrusted it with her mother to mail for her.

That night after dinner, when he found Marion and Edith alone in the cabin, he tried to engage Edith in conversation, but she ignored him completely and the next moment he bounded away up the companionway steps to the deck, frowning and muttering, "Oh hell! I guess she was looking forward to becoming Lady Draker at the Villa Rosa in Naples in the not far distant future. Well, there is nothing left for me to do upon my arrival in Grimsby than to wind up my affairs there and return to the States—and forget!"

"What's that, Jud?" asked Black Jack.

"Nothing, you lubber! I was just thinking aloud," Captain Beasley told him, grimly, as he began to pace the deck, his sea-green eyes gloom ridden.

Le Havre, France
Le Havre is situated in northwestern France on the right bank of the
river Seine on the English Channel.

37
HOMEWARD BOUND

The trip back to Grimsby, via Le Havre, was a long and tiresome
one for all hands. It was more so for the delicate creatures in the
cabin. When off Cape Verde, a tropical storm sent the girls below deck.
The officers aft were wondering how they fared. They imagined all
were sick but Edith and were lying in their berths until they heard them
singing. When Edith broke out into song, the men fore and aft stood
riveted to the deck. Jud commented, "I have an idea that Edith and
Marion stilled their fears and got them all together singing, but did you
ever hear so lovely a voice? I guess Edith surprised all those girls.
Listen to them now jabbering away!" he suggested.

When off Cape Finisterre, they ran into dirty weather again. The
Jenny was scudding along under fore-staysail, double-reefed fore and
main, for twenty-four hours to the westward. And, while the decks
were flooded occasionally, the little schooner rode the mountainous
waves like a duck, gliding into the hollows, then rising again and
shaking herself like a living thing.

Black Jack laughed at her antics as she dashed aside the waters of
the Atlantic. "My Jenny," he chortled, "how I do love you!"

"The ship or Victor's sister?" Jud asked.

"Both, you lubber!" he grinned.

"I daresay, I daresay," chuckled Victor, who was then thinking of
Marion.

When the storm lifted, Jud had all sails set and headed back toward
Le Havre, bucking against the northeaster all the way. There, he set the

girls ashore after Edith and Marion had spent a day shopping along the Rue St. Drapier for articles of apparel the girls needed. The parting was punctuated with sighs and tears and smiles and an hour later the schooner headed out to sea again, bound for Grimsby; that smelly, fishy town that the Jenny had left so many months before on what Black Jack had thought at the time was but a wild-goose chase.

As Jud sailed into the Humber on that June summer's day with all colors flying, the men broke out into song. The Barstow fleet had arrived that morning from the North Sea and was preparing to depart again. The welcome extended them one could not forget. After the Jenny left Le Havre, Jud had found an opportunity to have a chat with the Belle of Grimsby alone, while Marion was up on deck with Victor, a lubber who had declared he would never marry in the days gone by. He had popped the question to the girl before the schooner had even left the Gulf of Guinea and was accepted, the girl telling him that she had become a fatalist, like Captain Beasley. She knew then why she had to be abducted. If she had not, she would never had met the man she loved so dearly and would have died an old maid. Victor had replied, "Stop funning, Marion, darling. You don't have to marry a smelly fisherman."

"I do. I want to. I love fish!" she had told him in the presence of Edith who had smiled at them, knowing that they loved each other with all their hearts and souls, but, she herself, was a very unhappy girl at that moment.

Edith was asking Captain Beasley why he had not answered her letters. He stated he had never heard from her. She told him that before leaving Grimsby after she and her mother had laid her grandmother to rest, she had entrusted one with her mother to leave with Mrs. Jenson. He said if he had received that letter he would not have left Grimsby as he had, after he and Victor had been released from gaol. He asked her if she had believed the lying reports about him and his friend, Victor Jenson, having waylaid and robbed their friend, Black Jack Barstow.

"Certainly not!" she had declared.

"You believed Draker's lying reports that Jim Barkley and I had gone ashore at Funchal to have a jollification with the wenches there?" he questioned.

"I did not!" she assured him, heatedly.

"You believed that I went to the castle on the hill for the same purpose?"

"No, Jud. I did not!"

"Good Lord, Edith, what did you or do you believe?"

"I do not believe that my mother had any part in tricking me into taking that trip on the Angel Girl with the countess and Sir Henry."

"I see. You boarded her of your own free will to go along with them and from the gulf to Naples to marry Sir Henry at the Villa Rosa. I understand," he said, bitterly.

"How ridiculous! Nothing was farther from my thoughts. How on earth could you believe for one moment that my dear mother..."

"Wait!" he interrupted. "I do believe that," he asserted, emphatically. "Mr. Barkley, the mate, overheard the conversation between Lady Moresby and her dear friend Sir Henry. When I left Grimsby, I intended calling on you at Oak Lodge. Upon my arrival there, I saw in the lobby a paper published by Sir Richard Tracy. After reading this article," he said, taking the clipping from his pocket, "I decided it would be useless and—and left for the port of Funchal hoping to meet that black devil face to face. I was going to question him in reference to the whereabouts of Captain Mort, that piratical slaver who I learned later was no other than the father of Sir Henry Mortimer Draker, who was living in that castle on the hill with a bevy of beautiful girls in his harem. What happened there in the gulf, you know. But, you see, I was fated to meet Jim Barkley, a man you knew, on the beach at Funchal who was then mate of the Angel Girl and who had come ashore looking for a second mate. The rest you know. How about that article?" he asked, grimly.

Edith had stared at her own picture and read the article beneath it with wide open eyes.

"It is a lie!" she burst out. "Had I seen it on that day, I would have called on Sir Richard Tracy and..."

He interrupted her, gently. "That trip would have availed you nothing, my dear. Sir Richard, his wife, and her mother, Lady Melville were sojourning in Europe. Your own mother could have answered your question to your entire satisfaction."

Tears had welled up in her lovely eyes.

"Do you mean to infer that my own mother had that notice placed in the paper?"

"I do! Furthermore, my dear, I accuse her of withholding your letters. I asked Jack if he had received any letters for me, addressed in his care. He did not! That letter, too, you had entrusted to your mother. Lady Moresby is responsible for the abduction of her lovely daughter, of destroying the letters entrusted to her, and of placing that article in the paper. I am quite positive of that fact, my dear."

"I won't believe it!" she persisted. "Leave me, please! I cannot bear more at this time."

Jud went up on deck frowning. When they landed in Grimsby, Edith fell into the arms of Victor's sister weeping.

Black Jack drove away with the three girls after telling Barkley, Victor, and Beasley they were expected to dinner that night. The three men proceeded to the Jenson home and prepared for the event. When they entered the big house on the hill, Black Jack blurted, "Edith left immediately for London, Jud."

"She did? Did she say when she was coming back? If not, then after I wind up all my affairs here and in London, disposing of that junk you saw in my sea chest I took from the Angel Girl, I shall be heading back to the States, my friends."

He stared at Jenny and asked her if Edith had told her she would be returning. She smiled sadly. "No, Jud. Not one word."

"Another chapter in my life is closed forever," Jud told his friends. "Yours and Victor's are in the offing. Captain Victor Jenson, the new owner of the schooner, 'Jenny,' he concluded, grimly. "and...."

Black Jack interrupted him, "And over the office door down there on the wharf will be a new sign reading, Barstow, Jenson, Barkley & Company."

Jud nodded, smiling faintly. Barkley asked, "Where does the company come in, Jack?"

Jud answered the question. "I guess he is counting the chickens before they are hatched, you lubber! He refers to the little Barstows, Jensons, and Barkleys, undoubtedly."

38
I'M GOING BACK TO GRIMSBY

"Mother dear," Edith was saying the following morning while at breakfast, "are you quite sure that you did not forget to leave my letter with Mrs. Jenson before we left Grimsby after my dear Grandma was laid to rest?"

"Quite sure, my darling!" Lady Moresby said, avoiding the penetrating gaze of her daughter's eyes.

"Are you quite sure you mailed the letter to Captain Judson Beasley in care of Black Jack Barstow?"

"Quite sure!" she replied, still avoiding the accusing eyes of her daughter that were filming over with tears at the moment.

"Are you quite sure, mother dear, that you had no part in tricking your daughter to board the Angel Girl that evening, several months ago?"

Never in all her life had Lady Moresby felt so uncomfortable, so unhappy before, since the death of her fisherman husband. Her perturbation knew no bounds. She rose from her chair, irritably. "Your questions, my child, are an insult. I forbid you to speak another word on that subject."

Edith knew her mother was lying. She placed the clipping that Jud had given her before her mother's eyes and asked, "Are you quite sure that it was not you who had that article published in Sir Richard Tracy's paper, without my consent?"

"This is terrible!" raged Lady Moresby. "You do not know what you are saying. Accusing your mother of …."

She could not go on. She stalked out of the dining room to the drawing room and dropped into a seat, sobbing bitterly, but Edith followed her and went on inexorably, "Upon my arrival in London yesterday before entering this house, mother, I called at the office of Sir Richard Tracy and asked who had placed this article in the paper. Sir Richard was not there, but the business manager looked it up and he said that Lady Barry and Lady Moresby had called and that you, mother dear, had stated that I wished it published. You have lied to me all along. You plotted with Sir Henry to starve me aboard the Angel Girl—to feed me on fish, fish, fish! That you knew I detested so much, telling him that I would get so sick of it that I would never care to see Jud or that smelly, fishy town of Grimsby again. You know that is true!"

She laughed, then went on sadly, her eyes filming over, "The night that Captain Victor Jenson boarded the Angel Girl, when we were in the Gulf of Guinea and dined with us as the guest of Sir Henry, I made up my mind to taste the smelly stuff. I enjoyed it immensely. I never could have believed it was so delicious. I love fish! Do you hear me? I love Grimsby and the fisher-folk there. I tell you that you have lied to me—that you would have sold your daughter, soul and body, to the devil, to the son of the man who hung Jud's father to the yard arm of the old Spitfire of which Sir Henry was mate under his father known as "Black Mort" of whose hellish exploits you read about in the years gone by. I shall give the story to Sir Richard Tracy," she told her sobbing mother, heatedly.

"Where is Sir Henry and the Countess?" Lady Moresby asked, still avoiding the tear-dimmed eyes of her daughter.

"Sir Henry, with his mistress, the Countess Catherine Du Bois, and her maid the slave girl, who was his mistress likewise, are dead. The schooner foundered in the Gulf of Guinea. (Marion had told her what Jud had said.)

"Dead! Surely you are…"

"No, mother. I am not lying. I am telling you the truth!"

Edith turned on her heel and went upstairs to her room. Later, dressed in a grey cloth traveling suit, she came down stairs and paused at the door to the drawing room and called, "My trunks will be called for immediately. I am going, mother dear…..I want you to know that I forgive you and love you. Goodbye!"

177

"Where are you going, my child?" asked Lady Moresby, her large blue eyes moist with suppressed tears.

"I'm going back to Grimsby. Where men are men, brave and true! Back to that smelly, fishy town I love so, mother. Goodbye!" she repeated.

When Lady Moresby recovered from her swoon, she went up to her boudoir and penned a long letter to her daughter, sending it in care of Lady Barstow. Never, in her life, since the death of her fisherman husband, had her lovely face, so like Edith's, been washed with tears as on that day.

Black Jack had told Jud that he was quite sure Edith would be writing and suggested that he should call there again before leaving for London. The night after Edith left Oak Lodge for Grimsby, he found himself up at the Barstow residence on the hill, where he expected her letter .

Lady Moresby admitted him, the maid being busy at the moment, but she avoided his gaze as she ushered him into the parlor and asked him to be seated.

"A letter from Edith?" he asked, wearily.

"No, Captain, but I have a present for you," she announced, her sunken, black eyes aglow as she excused herself and left him wondering.

He had barely been seated when the Belle of Grimsby, robed in a beautiful evening gown of pale blue silk, glided toward him with a sweet smile of welcome on her face and her hands extended, as he rose and gazed at the lovely vision before him. He was speechless, but his eyes were glowing.

"Jud, dear, I received a long letter from my mother asking us to return to Oak Lodge and be married at St. Paul's."

Still speechless, he caught her in his arms and held her close, kissing her. She gasped, "I wrote mother and told her that after we were married, here at St. James Church, we would pay her a visit before we leave for Paris."

"You did, you darling!"

"I did so, Jud, dear. When we return to Grimsby from our honeymoon trip, I daresay you will be going back to your fishing up in the North Sea, but you don't have to, Jud. You don't have to risk your life up there again. You see, Jud, my grandmother left me over thirty thousand pounds and I want you to use it, every penny of it, as best you may," she told him, smiling.

Do tell!" he laughed, happily. "Ha, ha, ha!" he roared, as he folded the Belle of Grimsby in his arms.

ABOUT THE AUTHOR

Patrick John Rose was born on board his father's ship, the Marguerite, off the coast of New York on January 29, 1872. His stories relate that his father's name was (Captain) John Wesley Rose of Dublin, Ireland. Patrick claimed to have sailed for more than 30 years and was familiar with the Grimsby Docks of England, Humber Estuary, and the Dogger Banks of the North Sea. Patrick was also familiar with Dacre Castle, which was being used (according to Wikipedia) as a farm home by 1816, later restored into an elegant private residence. Patrick professed to be a "sailor, prospector, miner, cowpoke, and oil worker." He published one book during his lifetime (Bitter River Ranch in 1936 through Phoenix Press) and wrote many others as well as painted numerous illustrations for his manuscripts—many of schooners—one of which purportedly hung in the White House. Records indicate that he was married and living in San Francisco by 1918. Patrick John "Stanley McShane" Rose died in August, 1959, in Long Beach near the ocean he loved at 87 years of age.

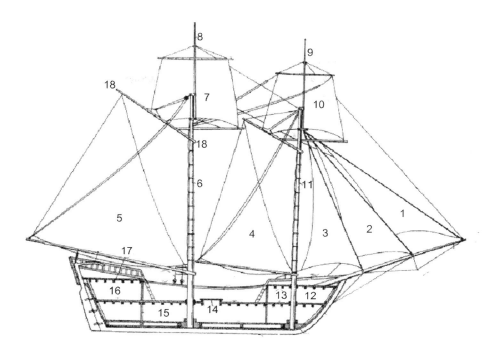

1   Flying Jib: the outermost of two or more jibs.
2   Jib: a foresail, triangle shaped sail forward of the mast. According to Wikipedia, the main halyard (for the mainsail) is fastened on the starboard side of the mast and the jib halyard to the port side.
3   Fore Staysail: the triangular foresail next forward of the mast.
4   Foresail: the sail being the lowest sail on the foremast.
5   Mainsail: the principal sail.
6   Main Topmast-The second mast is called the mizzen mast and the sail is called the mizzen sail. The mast immediately aft was called the Spanker, or mizzen spanker sail.
7   Mainsail
8   Gaff: a spar in a gaff rig.
9   Foremast
10 Fore Topsail
11 Yard: a spar fastened to the mast. The ends of a yard are yardarms.
12 Forecastle (fo'c'sle): Crew's quarters.
13 Main Deck
14 Captain's Cabin
15 Lazarette

16 Quarter Deck: part of the upper deck abaft the mainmast, including the poop deck. Break over the stern of the ship, or break of the poop.

17 Binnacle: According to Wikipedia, a binnacle is a waist-high stand on the deck of a ship, generally mounted in front of the helmsman, in which navigational instruments are placed for easy and quick reference. Its main purpose is to hold the ship's magnetic compass.

18 Each of the corners on a quadrilateral fore-and-aft rigged sail has its own name: The throat is the upper, forward corner of the sail. The peak is the upper aft corner.

19 Forestay: A wire or metal rod that runs from the bow to the top of the mast to provide support from the front. The backstay provides support from the opposite direction, and the shrouds provide support from each side.

20 Halyard: the line used to raise and lower the sail.

A **roadstead** is a place outside a harbor where a ship can lie at anchor.
Luff – to sail toward the wind.

SHIPS:

Barque: A sailing ship with from three to five masts, all of them square-rigged except the after mast, which is fore-and-aft rigged.
Coaster: A vessel engaged in coastal trade.
Ketch: A ketch is a sailing craft with two masts: a main mast, and a shorter mizzen mast abaft (rearward of) the main mast.
Lugger: A lugger is a class of widely used fishing sail boats, particularly off the coasts of France, England and Scotland.
Proa: A type of multihull native sailing vessel generally employing an outrigger.
Schooner: A schooner is a type of sailing vessel characterized by the use of fore-and-aft sails on two or more masts with the forward mast being no taller than the rear masts.
Yawl: A yawl is a two-masted sailing craft similar to a sloop or cutter but with an additional mast (or mizzen mast).

SHIPS IDENTIFIED WITHIN THIS BOOK

Angel Girl – schooner

Fanny Rawlings – barque

Good Hope - steamer

Jenny – schooner

Nancy Bell – "The Wreck of the Nancy Bell published in 1885 by
W. S. Gilbert.

Mary Jane – coasting lugger –sank in 1897

Spitfire – numerous ships under this name from row galley to clipper.

11808123R00108

Printed in Great Britain
by Amazon.co.uk, Ltd.,
Marston Gate.